TO LOVE AND DIE IN ATLANTA

VOL. 3

SA'ID SALAAM

URBAN AESOP PUBLICATIONS

"C-note in this bitch! One of y'all niggas get up!" C-note barked when barged into the prison barber shop. To his surprise his dad's protective custody had followed him down the road. Every one of the convicts who rode to prison with him had been flipped one way or another in the week they had been there.

One had become a Rider, two others had joined the Rollers. Both of the white men who rode with them were now white women. Walking around like Bruce Jenner in dresses and fake boobs. Meanwhile, no one dared to even look Carey's way. That's why when he received a slip to visit the barber shop he barged in like a bear.

"I got you player," a barber said and pulled the sheet from his half finished client.

"Man!" the man pouted as he sat down and waited to get the other half of his head cut. The banal barbershop banter resumed once Carey was seated. They talked about the usual subjects of pussy, drugs, money and murder. Subjects Carey knew all about.

"Shit, I prolly fucked more hoes than all y'all broke ass niggas put together!" he laughed. He always enjoyed talking down on people but it was even sweeter since they couldn't do anything about it. "Y'all niggas ain't never had no white girl head! Y'all niggas ain't no killers! I been knocking niggas off..."

Carey lost his train of thought and nearly choked on his next words when a familiar face walked into the barbershop. His presence was larger than life and pushed the rest of the men right out of the room. Carey tried to get up himself but the barber's strong arms easily held him in place.

"Un-uh, finish your story," the man said as he took a seat right in front of him.

"I, I, I mean," Carey stammered. Big Marquis looked so much like his son there was no question of who he was. What he didn't know was why he was here. "You know my dad said no one can touch me!"

"Nah, I spared you lil nigga," Marquis corrected and pulled a phone from his pocket. He placed his video call and leaned back. "Finish your story..."

"Hello?" Marquita asked and scrunched her face up when she saw her baby daddy on the phone. They didn't have a baby together anymore so she wondered why he was calling. She cast a glance out at her husband flipping steaks on the grill.

"Yeah, this nigga was just telling us about how he killed our kid," he explained. Marquita knew who he was and what was about to happen. She nodded her head and leaned in to watch.

Marquis gave the nod and the barber produced a straight razor. He started from one ear and pulled it around his neck to the other ear. Carey looked shocked but nothing happened for a few full seconds. The thin line suddenly opened up and blood gushed from the now gaping wound.

Carey made a gruesome, blood curdling sound as blood spewed down the barber's smock. Marquita didn't blink as she watched him struggle for life while the barber held him in place. The light in his eyes flickered before it went dark. His head dropped to his chest as his soul gurgled out from the wound.

"Make sure you tell my son who sent you. Fuck boy," Big Marquis snarled at the dead teen. Carey's eyes were wide open but he didn't see shit. Nor could he hear the parting words of the man who spared him just to watch him die. "I would have done it myself but I'm finna go home on early release."

"I got this mess shawty. Get on up out of here," the barber said of the crime scene. He had two life sentences without the possibility of parole so there wasn't much they could do to him.

"Yeah, cuz I'm finna hit that city and take err thang that's mine..." Marquis smiled that sinister smile of his.

CHAPTER ONE

"Are you sure?" Madelyn Worthington asked again as her daughter came downstairs with the first of many bags.

"I've never, ever been so sure of anything in my life!" Kelondra stopped in her tracks and declared with her whole soul. A strong sentiment from the wishy washy teen who usually couldn't make up her mind. She might order pizza but decide she wants sushi and leave before it arrives. Her parents could save her from her own impetuousness while she was home, but now she was about to leave.

"I just..." he mother moaned and searched for the right words. The right words would be vulnerable, fragile, delicate even, but Kelondra would have rebelled against those words. True as they were. Her daughter had endured more mental trauma than most grown people could take.

Divorce of parents has sent many kids to the dark side in itself. Kelondra didn't have time to recover since her brother was murdered shortly after. To add insult to injury her boyfriend switched up on her and left her to deal with it on her own. Marquis Williams slid into her life like a stolen base and made her feel safe. Until Carey blew his brains all over her face.

Kelondra still graduated with honors but only because she was so far ahead she was able to coast the rest of the way through the school year. She couldn't remember a single word spoken at graduation since her mind was elsewhere. The summer was a blur. Her mother kept her busy with a flurry of activities to keep her mind busy. They only served to keep her body busy because her mind was encased in a capsule of grief.

Her mother was right though and staying home while attending freshman classes would be the best thing for her. Dorm life was not for the weak minded, soft hearted or gullible. Eighteen year olds just like her were coming from a variety of cities and states. They brought with them the baggage and customs they were accustomed to in their own homes and hometowns. Geeks, freaks and chic all stirred into one pot was a recipe for disaster.

The prestigious school had an exorbitant price to ensure only the cream of the financial crop could afford to send their offspring. Which of course came with a whole host of other problems since rich people never equates to good people. A lot of rich people climbed the ladder of success on the heads of the less fortunate people.

Others worked so hard for the money they didn't get to raise their children. They had virtual strangers living in their houses and eating their food. Some business people were ruthless and fucked up who raised ruthless, fucked up kids.

Plus, whoever thought it was a good idea to put hundreds

of grown children alone in a building with no supervision really fucked that one up. If not for the percentage of good kids, from good homes, with good parents all would be lost like the Minnow. Kelondra was a good kid, who came from a good home but that home also produced Kenneth 'Keto' Williams. So it could go either way.

Madelyn herself came from a good home, with good parents. Besides getting a little loose in her sophomore year she made out pretty good. She met her husband in junior year and never looked back.

"Just what mother?" Kelondra asked impatiently, but respectfully when her mother drifted away into her own head. A medley of memories put a slight smirk on her face as she recollected the good times of her freshman year. The drinks, the drugs, the dicks and even a vagina.

"I just want what's best for you," she sighed and shook it off.

"Oh, I know what this is about!" the daughter nodded and pointed at her mother as they stood in the middle of the nearly four thousand foot house that had been their home. Home is where the family is but now the family was gone. "You're going to be here all alone!"

"Um, yes. That's it," Madelyn agreed and switched gears. If this angle would keep her home she would gladly go with it. "First your dad. Then Kenneth and now you're leaving me!"

"I'm just going to school mom!" she shrieked at the comparisons. Her dad ran off with a young girl while her brother was dead and buried. "I'm thirty minutes away in the city!"

"I know. I'm sorry," the woman sighed. She may have

been able to guilt trip her father and ex husband into bending to her whims but she inadvertently raised a daughter with the same wiles.

Kelondra had a sex appeal that she had yet to discover herself. The aire of innocence about her made her even more desirable. Even when she adopted her 'Ki-ki' persona it was still relatively tame. If, or when she realized the power of femininity she could be dangerous. Once she discovered the power of the P she would rule the world. Or at least the world that surrounded her.

"Well, I'll follow you down and help you get settled," Madelyn offered in defeat.

"It's not kindergarten mom!" Kelondra fussed.

"No dear, it's your freshman year of college. And I'm going to escort you to the dorm just like my mom and dad did when I went to school," she replied back in a tone that left no room for debate.

"I wonder where dad is?" she asked since they had discussed this day in happier days.

"Probably..." Madelyn was saying with some harsh words on the tip of her tongue but movement outside stole her attention. Her lips twisted when she saw who was pulling into the driveway. "Pulling up now."

"Daddy!" the daddy's girl cheered and took off through the door. Her mother scrunched her face in disgust at what she perceived to be treason. She did her best to instill the fact that her husband didn't just leave her, he left the whole family.

Which was her right since she was right. She had been a good wife who kept a clean house and vagina. She doted over her kids and fucked her husband at will. Cooked, cleaned and laughed at corny jokes. There was no reason for him to leave her, or them. Except for his own selfish desires. Her attempts to spice up their love life just couldn't complete with the plethora of pussy in the city of Atlanta.

"Hey baby girl!" Kenneth Worthington cheered back and threw his arms open for a hug. He used to be Kenneth senior until his junior got killed. Now his daughter was all he had left. For now since his new wife was only a few years older than her.

"I knew you wouldn't miss it!" she bounced as her mother came out of the house.

"Not for the world," he said and held up the key fob to the electric Audi he pulled up in. The girl hadn't noticed the new car until just that second. Her mother did since she craned her neck to see if Kendra was inside. She wanted to finish the brawl she started at the funeral.

"Thank you! Thank you! Thank you!" she cheered and bounced some more.

"What about the perfectly fine car she was driving?" Madelyn hissed. He bought that one too but she needed something to bitch about.

"I traded it for the new one. I'll follow her down and take it with me," he explained to her while watching his daughter fawn over her new car. A pang in his heart made him wince since he was supposed to have bought two cars. His wife seemed to sense the same thing and fell back.

"Well, let's get this caravan on the road," Madelyn suggested. Everyone got into their vehicle for the short ride over to another world.

ATLANTA TECH WAS the most prestigious school in the city. People only settle for UGA, Georgia state and Georgia tech if they couldn't get in. Even their dorm was a high rise condo building. Units could fetch half a million on the open market if they hadn't been diced up into dorms.

The parking lot was a flurry of activity from the students moving in. The school staggered the move in days by class and today was for the freshman class. They would occupy the lower floors with each class ascending upward above the skyline. Mainly because freshmen were more likely to jump.

There was a vivid array of colors and hues as the students began to arrive. Green was the dominant color here since whoever could afford the ticket and had the grades was welcome. Still, that made for a fifty percent Caucasian student body. Thirty percent African American while other races filled in the other percent.

The high ticket price kept the school exclusive but federal law made them inclusive since they had to offer scholarships to inner city students from inner cities from around the country. That's how Vonda made it.

"Dang!" Sheronda exclaimed as she pulled up to the building.

"I know mama!" the girl gasped while looking up to the top of the building. Her mother had been protesting about her going away for school so she hoped seeing the dorm would change her tune.

"Still don't see why you tryna go to no damn college!" the woman fussed again. "Who supposed to help me with yo brothers and sisters?"

"Um, how 'bout they daddies?" she shot back to remind her that they weren't her responsibility. Being a built-in babysitter was one of her main reasons to leave the house. Each baby had a different baby daddy except the twins but only because they were twins. Still, five baby daddies for her six kids. "That's a lot of manpower!"

"A'ight now..." the woman warned at the sass. "What about our 'biz-niss?"

"Shoot, look at this place mama!" Vonda reminded and waved her hand around the parking lot. "All these rich folks. Shoot we finna tear they ass up!"

The Perry were a family of boosters, scammers, thieves and con artists. Sheronda Perry also slung a little ass on the side when needed. A win/win for a woman who loved dick as much as she loved money. And she loved money plenty even though it was the root of all of her evil.

The mother had to nod her head and agree with all the potential victims moving about. She would pay to be able to slither around in this building but instead they were paying her daughter to do the same. The scholarship and stipend covered the price of admission but a degree itself would be priceless. Vonda was ready to go straight in life, if her mama would let her. Or, her infatuation with the finer things didn't keep her distracted.

She quickly unloaded her belongings from the trunk and sat them on the curb. Nothing was left behind since she never intended to return home. Plus two of her younger sisters had filled out enough to wear her clothes. She left them whatever she couldn't fit in her bags. Plus they went in her bag and stole a few things they wanted. The Perry house was a free for all. You had to hide your money, food and clothing or it was fair game.

"I see some fine youngins 'round here!" Sheronda grunted as she sweated the student body's student bodies.

"Mama you need to pull off. Remember this car is hot," Vonda reminded. The last thing she wanted was her mother getting arrested in the parking lot on move in day.

"Borrowed! But you right," she agreed and got back into the car. It's owner was still sleeping in her bed since she slipped him a Mickey when she brought him home. The poor fellow just wanted a little pussy and didn't mind paying for it. He got a little pussy but it was costing him a lot more than he bargained for. She took his wallet with the credit and debit cards. Plus his drivers license and social security card to steal his whole identity.

Her other teen girls, twins, Panda and Miranda peeled his jewelry off while he slept. The seventeen year olds giggled while they played with his dick and took pictures of it. Their fifteen year old brother named Kirby hacked into his phone and worked the Cash Apps and PayPal until they locked up. He was going to wish he stayed home with his wife once they were through with his ass.

"I'll help..." a male student said when he saw Vonda struggling. He grabbed a few bags before she could protest and she was grateful for the help.

"Thanks!" she offered sincerely ahead as she checked him out from behind.

"My pleasure," he smiled and held the door for her.

"Ok then!" Vonda cheered. It was only the first day and she could get used to bougie life already. She found her unit on the second floor and realized her new roommate had already arrived. She summoned a smile as she walked in and introduced herself. "Hello! I'm Vonda Perry!"

"Kelondra Worthington!" Kelondra replied and shook her hand.

CHAPTER TWO

"Well, let's leave these girls to get acquainted," Madelyn suggested when she saw her ex husband eyeing Vonda's thick caramel thighs under the mid thigh skirt.

"Huh?" he asked since the caramel thighs under the mid thigh skirt had him stuck for a moment. The words caught up a split second later and he agreed. "Oh, ok. Ok baby girl, you call me if you need anything!"

"Thank you dad!" she thanked for the offer as well as the thick roll of hundreds he withdrew from his pocket. He and Vonda counted out ten of them before he passed them off to her.

"Anytime," he said to them both and cast the other girl a glance that meant she could call too. "Let me go turn this car in..."

"Yeah," Madelyn agreed as she came out behind him. She wanted to say something slick but no words came to mind at the moment.

"Nice parents!" Vonda gushed once they were alone.

"I guess," the spoiled girl shrugged. "Did your parents come?"

"Huh?" she asked for an answer since her daddy was still an unanswered question. Her mama was riding around in a semi stolen car and she was pretty sure she didn't want to reveal that. "Yeah, they just left. Busy, work and stuff."

Kelondra wasn't paying much attention to the answer since she was far too self centered to care about what other people thought or said. Some questions were just courteous to ask even if she didn't care about the answer. She did feel the heat of her watching as she put her clothes into the drawers. Vonda was counting her clothes just like she counted her daddy's pocket.

"Where are you from?" Vonda asked. She saw enough designer labels to know she wasn't from any hood. Even though she had a few of those same labels she was pretty sure Kelondra didn't boost them like she did.

"West View. It's thirty minutes north of here," she explained. A lot of people didn't know about the exclusive enclave until recent events thrust them into the spotlight.

"Oh yeah! That's where that basketball player got kilt!" she exclaimed. She heard the hood come out and quickly swept it back under the rug. "Killed. He was shot."

"He was my boyfriend," she sighed and twisted her lips. She had been doing well today but the weight now pulled her down on her bed. She sat down and let out another deep sigh.

"I'm sorry girl!" Vonda moaned. She felt bad that her question led to the girl feeling bad. She knew what would make her feel better so she offered. "Want a Perc?"

Kelondra stared at the pill in her hand for seconds that

felt like minutes. She had taken them before and knew they would make her feel better. She also had seen them send enough of her classmates to rehab too. The weight of pros and cons can shift according to the moment so at this moment it seemed like a good idea.

Vonda had a few to sell but didn't use them herself. Her family life and upbringing were enough of a handicap. She wouldn't saddle herself with drugs, alcohol or even nicotine. There was more she didn't do than did do, especially coming from where she came from. Southwest Atlanta was only a few miles away but it may as well have been on a different planet than the one she was on now.

"Thanks," Kelondra sang and popped the pill dry. They both looked over at the apartment size fridge in the kitchen, but it was empty. She used a gulp of saliva to get it down and made a suggestion. "Guess we need to shop?"

"Facts!" Vonda agreed even though she only had a hundred dollars to her name. The stipend was cool but not enough for her to live on and dress nice. Like it or not she was going to have to get on her hustle soon.

"WHAT THE, WHERE THE..." the naked man wondered when he wandered awake in the strange room. He felt the hot

body next to him that was just as naked as he was. His face strained as he strained to remember what happened that got him here. His dull headache throbbed when he tried to think.

"Mmmm, daddy!" Sheronda moaned and leaned her hot

body against his. She had worked him for all she could and slid back into the bed when he awoke around noon after dropping her daughter off at college.

"Hey?" he asked when he saw her face. He vaguely recalled meeting her and coming home with her. "Did we..."

"Did we!" she laughed and cheered. She gripped his dick and gave it a good squeeze as a reminder. It quickly throbbed to life and got stiff in her hand.

"One for the road?" he suggested and pulled her on top of him. His watch was missing so he looked over to the clock that misread the time. He needed to get home by nine but nine was hours ago.

"Mmhm," Sheronda cooed and grinded her hot box on the shaft of his dick. Soon she was slick and slippery so he reached down and worked himself inside. To her credit each of her baby daddies made the decision to fuck her raw so no one could ever claim she trapped them.

"Shit!" he cussed cuz squeezing into some good, hot pussy makes you cuss. He gripped her nice, round ass cheeks and thrusted deep inside of her. The bed began to squeak when he threw it into overdrive.

The youngest two Perry kids snickered and giggled from the cracked doorway. The six and seven year olds always got a kick out of mama letting men hunch on her. Kirby on the other hand hated hearing the sounds of sex coming from his mother's room. Even if he did charge the man's accounts while he humped.

"Mmhm!" Sheronda grunted when he began to writhe underneath her. She knew by the look on his face he wouldn't last much longer. That's why she pinned his wrist to bed and leaned her weight on the dick.

"Up, up!" he urged since he didn't want to bust in some strange pussy. It would have made more sense not sliding into some strange pussy raw but a hard dick and sense ain't never been close.

"Un-uh!" she declined and finished him off with a squeeze of that hot box. She nearly cracked up when he squirmed and made faces as he exploded inside of her. Shit may have felt good now but it was going to cost him a thousand dollars for the abortion she would not have to have since her tubes were tied, singed and twisted.

"Shit!" he fussed as she milked him dry with her muscles and movement. When she let up his flaccid dick fell out and laid on his stomach. "I gotta get home?"

"Yeah," she agreed as he searched for his drawers. His wallet and phone were back where he left them since they had already been raided. Even his phone was in the pocket he left it, along with his car keys. "Call me?"

"Sure, yeah! Sure!" he lied and rushed out of the house. He didn't even notice his car was still warm from Sheronda running errands all morning while he slept. He would now have his hands full trying to stop the leaking from his accounts. As soon as he did Sheronda would hit him up for abortion money.

He got a little pussy alright, but it sure cost a lot.

"SHIT!" Vonda shrieked when they reached the checkout line. She frantically checked her purse, then pockets.

"What's wrong?" Kelondra asked, matching her urgency.

She looked around too even though she had no idea what they were looking for.

"My wallet! I can't find..." she said and paused to check again. "My wallet! It's gone!"

"Oh no!" Kelondra moaned. She had lost a wallet once upon a time and knew how much work it meant to get identification cards and bank cards and social security cards.

"Shoot, how I'm supposed to pay for my stuff!" she pouted like she was about to cry. The cashier winced and scratched her head since she had seen this movie before. Enough times to know exactly how it ended.

"Don't worry about it! I got you!" Kelondra said, coming to her rescue.

"You for real?" Vonda asked like a really good actress. She knew she would pay, which was why there were two hundred dollars worth of items in her cart, when she only had a hundred dollars to her name.

"Sure! I got you V!" she sang happily. Not having a sister made her open to accepting her.

"Thank you sis!" Vonda sang and hugged her neck. The cashier rolled eyes and twisted her lips at the obvious hustle. Vonda just wished she had gotten a little more. The best way to milk a cow is slowly so she would go slow. And Kelondra had plenty judging by the brand new electric Audi they rode in. "Shoot!"

"What's wrong?" Kelondra needed to know now. She had become quite the nurturer after years of raising her twin brother and comforting her mother after the divorce. Now fixing other people's problems has become second nature.

"Nothing," her friend pouted and batted her eyes like she might just burst into tears.

"You sure?" she pleaded so she could fix it.

"My wallet, and I'm hungry!" the scammer explained.

"Oh girl, don't worry about that! I got you!" the victim assured. By the time they got back to the dorm she had been bilked out of a couple hundred dollars more.

"I DON'T KNOW ABOUT THIS..." Kelondra hummed and twisted her lips to help her think. For some strange reason twisting lips is a part of the decision making process.

"What's not to know? Free party. Free drinks," Vonda read from the flier circulating around campus. She was sold on the word free since her mother taught her to try to get through life on the next person's dime. Plus she had never been to a college party before and couldn't wait to add the experience to her resume of life. Life is short so fill that muhfucka up as much as possible.

Kelondra on the other hand was all partied out after Marquis got killed. The last party she attended ended with her boyfriend's brains on her lap so she wasn't so eager to go to another. High school had one series of parties back in West view. She was here to learn, even if Atlanta Tech was officially the partying college Capital of the city known for partying.

"College boys..." Vonda added and wiggled her perfectly manicured brows.

"Yeah but, I don't know..." Kelondra moaned. She had climbed the fence but needed a little push to be convinced. The Perc she took earlier had eased her mind. A little music, weed, and a few beers might be just what the doctor ordered.

"Guess I can't go either then," her roommate pouted and plopped down on the sofa with her bottom lip poked out.

"You can!" Kelondra assured her.

"Nuh-uh. We besties, I'm not going nowhere without you sis!" she vowed. Now it was Kelondra's turn to pout at the sentiment.

"Awe! Gee, thanks!" she moaned. Once upon a time Katie used to be her bestie but now they didn't even speak. Her lips twisted once again but only for a second before a smile straightened them back up. It would be kinda nice to break 'Ki-ki' out and have some fun. "Let's ride!"

"You for real!" Vonda gushed like she was surprised. What did surprise her was that it took this long to convince the girl to do what she wanted her to do.

"Hells yeah! Let's go have some fun!" she cheered. They both retreated to their separate bedrooms with ensuite bathrooms. They showered the shopping trip away and got dressed.

Most college parties are college kid casual but the promoter billed this as a black tie affair. After all, this school was for the cream of various crops. Why not dress up to get drunk and fall down. Vonda had been to her share of hood parties where people got fucked up and fell down. She saw the drugs, the sex and violence but had never experienced how rich kids partied. Pretty much the same except no gangs, or shooting. There was the occasional fight but murders were rare. It had been Kelondra's bad luck to witness one of the very few.

"Killing this shit!" Vonda proclaimed when she inspected herself in the knockoff Gucci tube dress. It was boosted from a store that specializes in knockoff designer labels. The high heeled shoes came from Payless so she paid for them. A quick twirl of her curling iron put big, bouncy curls in her thick black hair.

Vonda smoothed her hands over her luscious lady lumps as she admired herself in the full length mirror. It wasn't a competition but then again it wasn't not a competition either. She genuinely liked Kelondra but still wanted to outshine her. Plus, Kelondra was a bad bitch herself so she definitely didn't want to be outshined.

"Wow! You look great!" Kelondra cheered, causing Vonda to cheese. Note to chicks, get friends who cheer for you.

"Dang! You too!" she shot back and admired the mid thigh Prada dress. The top dipped enough to show a couple pounds of good titty meat. She came closer to inspect and realized the dress was real. "This is nice!"

"Thanks. They hook me up down at Walden's," she said of the luxury store.

"Always wanted to go there," Vonda admitted before she could stop herself. She did stop before admitting she would tear their asses up if she did go in there. Boosting from the mall was easy compared to the high end stores like Walden's.

"You can come with me next time I go. Just let me know!" she assured and they headed out to go party.

"Mmhm," she hummed and nodded. Her phone buzzed as they headed out of the dorm. She debated on whether or not she should take her mother's call for a second, then took it. "Hey mama."

"Girl come home. I got us a lick!" she urged. Sheronda had copied the keys to a dope boys condo while he was sleeping. Now needed her to clean him out while they went out.

Panda and Miranda were too silly to pull it off by themselves. The goofy girls would get sidetracked, play with stuff
and take pictures in the crime scene.

"I cain't. Me and my roomy finna hit a party!" she
declined while Kelondra attempted to mimic her country
grammar.

'I cain't, I'm finna...' she practiced. She loved how her
new friend could turn it off and on at will.

"Shit, where the party at then? I'm finna fall through!"
Sheronda switched gears. She had the keys so she could
always hit him up later.

"It's for college kids!" she shrieked at the thought of her
mother in there twerking on her head. Sheronda could pass
for a junior since she wasn't much older than most grad
students. Birthing all them kids couldn't hurt that hourglass
figure in the least. If anything her ass was fatter and breast
heavier.

"You tryna say yo mama look like an old lady!" she fussed
playfully.

"No, you just look like someone auntie!" Vonda shot back
and cackled. Kelondra smiled and wished she and her
mother could cackle together. "Don't worry tho, I'm finna get
some numbers!"

"Ok then," Sheronda sighed and clicked off. All that
party talk had her ready to shake her ass so she dressed for a
night on the town as well.

"I should get a few numbers myself!" Kelondra declared.
Vonda just smiled and nodded even though they were on
different pages. The prissy girl was thinking cute coed phone
numbers while the ghetto girl was after dates of birth and
social security numbers.

CHAPTER THREE

"This is nice!" Vonda declared as they entered the frat house hosting the party. People had to move sideways to move around since it was jam packed.

"Mmhm," Kelondra practiced sounding like her. She spotted the makeshift bar and began squeezing her ways towards it.

"Get yo hand off my ass nigga!" Vonda barked at a drunken white guy who had drunk enough to think it would be a good idea to grab her ass.

"My bad!" he proclaimed and raised his hands in surrender. A broad smile stretched across his reddish face at being called the n-word. He and his friends back in Kansas used it on each other but having an actual black person call them one was a badge of honor.

"No problem!" she smiled but only because she was able to lift his wallet during the exchange. Once she lifted the cash and identification she would discard the rest. Only because she didn't know the value of the designer wallets rich kids carried.

"Ah yes!" Kelondra cheered when she received the big bowl of infamous 'jungle juice'. There is no standard recipe for the heavily loaded concoction as long as they had you swinging through the trees like Tarzan.

"Um, no thanks," Vonda grimaced and shook her head. She smoked a little weed once but drew the line at harder drugs and alcohol. Her mother hadn't taught her much good beyond steering clear of hard drugs and alcohol. They were the tools of their trade to rob suckers.

Vonda needed a bathroom pit stop to rummage through the wallets she lifted. She folded the cash into her purse and took pictures of ID and social security cards. Kirby would work them for all they were worth once he got them. They made their way out to the back yard that was a lot less crowded.

"Whoo hoo!" Ki-ki howled as she danced between two guys. It was clear she was swinging from the trees by now. It was also clear from the looks in their eyes they had something sinister in mind. Vonda kept a close eye on her friend until someone stole her attention.

"Well hello there," a voice called from beside her. Guys had been shooting their shots since she arrived but she shooed them away like flies. She glanced up to dismiss this one too but got stuck.

"Heeeeyyyy," Vonda sang and twirled her curls with her fingers when she saw the jet black beauty standing over her . She almost called him Amestad but let it pass. He took her smile as an invitation to sit, and sat.

"I'm Idris," he greeted and extended his large hand. Vonda tilted her head at it as if unsure what to do with it. Men and women didn't shake hands where she came from.

"Victoria, Vonda," she stammered in between her club name and her real name. She had never been to a real club but already had a club name she used in the streets. She laughed at his confusion and cleared it up. "Vonda."

"Nice to meet you," he smiled a bright smile that shines even brighter against his black skin. She was used to come-ons and sexual solicitations but he just kicked it and had her full attention. Vonda alternated between smiling at him and keeping an eye on her roommate.

"Wait!" Vonda interrupted when she saw another couple dancing where her friend and the couple of guys had just been.

"What's wrong?" Idris asked as she hopped up and looked around. She didn't hear him when she tore off in search of her friend.

"Move! Ki-ki! Ki-ki! Hands off!" she called out as she waded through the thick pool of people back inside. She just caught a glance of the two guys half carrying the highly intoxicated girl up the stairs. She moved with even more urgency to catch up.

It took a full few minutes to reach the stairs, then another minute to squeeze her way up. People were dancing, posting up and making out the whole way up. Reaching the top of the stairs was just half the battle since the hallway stretched both ways. Her head whipped back and forth trying to decide which way to go. Instinct said left so left she went. She opened the first door and saw one man screwing her friend on the bed while the other stood by naked for his turn.

"Get off of her!" Vonda screamed and snatched the man out of snatch.

"What the fuck!" the girl on the bed protested at the interruption.

"Oops! My bad!" Vonda laughed when she realized it was the wrong girl in the wrong room. She gave a wave as she backed out of the room. She stole a glance at each dick as she did. "As you were..."

She kept rushing into rooms and cock-blocking until she found Kelondra. She was nearly naked on a bed, snoring lightly. Lightly enough not to disturb the man between her legs lapping at her labia while the other filmed it on his phone. The camera man looked over while the one eating only lifted his eyes. Vonda just blinked for a second to process what she was seeing.

"Get up! Un-uh! Oh hell naw!" she fussed when she sprang into action. That meant snatching the phone from one man and kicking the other off her friend.

"My phone!" he protested as if that were more pressing than the sexual assault in progress.

"Fuck yo phone!" she dared and took a fighter's stance. "I'll use it to call the damn cops!"

"Fuck the phone!" the friend agreed and hit the door. His friend reluctantly followed and left the girls alone.

"Come on lil mama. I got you," Vonda said as she pulled her dress down from her neck.

"Hey girl. Whoo hoo!" Kelondra cheered and pumped her fist.

"Girl..." Vonda laughed and shook her head as she helped her up and out of the room. They made it to the steps before Kelondra's stomach revolted and expelled the liquor. She sprayed the party people on the stairs with jungle juice and pizza. Vonda got a good laugh out of that. "Whoo hoo!"

"YOU READY?" Vonda asked when Kirby answered the phone.

"Yup!" the boy wonder of hackers nodded as the pictures began coming in. Each name and social could be good for tens of thousands of dollars depending on credit. She stood to make a thousand each on each for her cut. The ten identities could net an easy ten grand. It could be more but Sheronda had to get her cut. "That's it?"

"Um..." she hummed and looked at the pictures of Kelondra's identity. Her virgin credit could be worked for years in his hands. She looked over at the sleeping girl's bedroom door and made a decision. Her head began to shake left to right before the words left her mouth. "Yeah, for now."

"I'll holla," Kirby said and clicked off. Vonda left her room to check on her friend. She had copied her info when she put her in bed last night but deleted it on the way over.

"Hey girl..." she said as she poked her head into the door.

"Ouch!" Kelondra moaned when she stirred awake the next afternoon. Her head felt like it was in a vice with a marching band beating inside of it.

"I bet!" Vonda laughed and opened her blinds to let the sun shine in.

"Ouch!" she repeated and winced at the bright light.

"Mmhm, that's how I felt when I couldn't find my future baby daddy last night!" she protested. Vonda had watched and waited for Idris after getting her in the car but he was nowhere to be found.

"Did we have fun last night?" Kelondra wondered since she certainly couldn't remember.

"Well, depends on what you consider fun..." Vonda smiled while pulling up the video. She turned the screen to let her see herself getting violated.

"Someone is getting their freak on..." Kelondra laughed when the video started. The smile flipped when she recognized the woman on the bed as herself. She strained her face trying to remember consenting until one of the men spoke up and put it in perspective.

"Go to sleep drunk, wake up pregnant!" the one behind the camera laughed. The two predators didn't even use protection since their victims never protested.

"She's got a pretty pussy!" the other declared and moved aside so he could film it. He fondled it and spread it for the camera. Kelondra grimaced at her private parts made public.

"Taste it!" the previous owner of the phone urged. His friend leaned in to comply but she had seen enough of the scene. Now she crossed her arms over her chest in shame.

"Turn it off!" Kelondra fussed and turned away.

"Nah..." Vonda refused and let it run until she barged in and saved her. Kelondra just blinked, then looked up gratefully.

"Thank you," Kelondra croaked. She just realized how close she came to getting date raped. Plenty of students went to sleep drunk and woke up pregnant at colleges all across the nation.

"These other hoes ain't make out so well..." she said and flipped through the various videos of the variety of vaginas in their collection.

"They need to pay for this!" Kelondra huffed indignantly.

"Oh, they 'fi'in-to," Vonda vowed. She would see to it since she had access to a wealth of information on the phone.

She would do to his credit what he planned to do to her friend. A financial rape without the date.

'Fi'in-to', Kelondra repeated in her head. She needed some real hood authenticity to make her Ki-ki persona more authentic.

"WHERE YOU HEADED?" Kelondra asked when Vonda came from her room and headed for the door. They had become even closer over the past few weeks so it was rare for one to go without the other. Except for classes.

"I gotta go to the house and talk to my brother," she said without breaking stride.

"Want me to drive you?" she offered since she had to drive them everywhere they went any other time. Except when Vonda went home since she always took an Uber.

"Naw, I'm cool. I'll see you later," she replied and rushed out the door so they wouldn't have to keep talking about it.

Vonda wouldn't necessarily say she was ashamed of her family but she certainly wasn't eager to show them off either. Not in her quest to go legit and be respectable. Her family of scammers would send the exact opposite message. She had been ducking her mother's request for licks but had now been summoned.

Sheronda gave the ultimatum to come home or she would come up to the school. The last things she needed in life was her ratchet mother and hood rat sisters running around the campus. Shit would get stolen and broken and she would get the blame.

"Sup cutie pie?" the driver smiled through the rear view

when Vonda climbed into the back seat. He got a nice glimpse of yellow panties when she slid inside.

"Y'all prices is what's up!" she snarled back and closed her legs. He began to talk some more but she had a better idea. "Can you turn that up?"

"Huh? Oh," he said and turned up the Doobie Daddie and Erv-G duet playing on the radio. He didn't stop talking but couldn't be heard over the radio.

Vonda felt her mood sour with the scenery as the landscape went from chic to bleak. The same sun shone overhead yet the hood seemed a little darker than where she just came from. It was hard to believe the same places existed on the same planet yet alone the same city.

"Here you are," the driver announced just in case she didn't know her house when she saw it.

"A'ight," she acknowledged and tried to guard her crotch as she slid back out. She watched his eyes in the rearview seek a peek. He extended a card to her once she got out of his vehicle. "What's this for?"

"Shit, I'ma driver. Holla when you need a ride. Ion have surge hours like them folk," he explained like a true hustler. He didn't mind driving for peanuts since he would solicit those same riders to go through him directly. He could charge less and still make more. True hustler for real.

"Check," she nodded and accepted the card. One thing her mama taught her was to have a network. Not necessarily a network of niggas and nigga-in-laws, but drivers, artist, cooks, etc. Her mama also taught her to say thank you so she put a little extra sway in her hips to thank him as she walked into the house.

"Vonda here!" six year old Shay sang. She and seven year old David rushed to be first to hug her neck.

"Hey y'all!" Vonda greeted and laughed as her siblings squeezed her. As bad as she wanted to, and needed to get away from this house she still missed her brothers and sister. Her mother not so much.

"A'ight, y'all turn her loose! Y'all lil niggas don't hug me like that!" Sheronda spat, jealously. "I'm the one pushed y'all out my pussy!"

"Eww!" Shay grunted and grimaced, while David snickered. The little porn addict was destined to be a freak when he grew up.

"Hey V!" the twins greeted as one as they came from their shared room.

"Um hey, but what y'all got on?" Vonda wanted to know. She scrunched up her face to let them know what she thought of the tiny little short sets they were wearing.

"Shorts!" Panda giggled and pulled them out of her crotch. An exercise in futility since the tiny shorts crept right back up between her legs as soon as she got them out.

"They good! Don't be acting all bougie now cuz you in that bougie school with all them bougie folk!" he mother snarled. She would never admit to being jealous of her first born but that's exactly what it was. The girl was thriving in a world she could never fit in so she had to hold on to control for as long as she could. Even she knew those days were counting down until she couldn't.

"Hey Kirby!" Vonda greeted as her nerdy brother came out from his lab.

"Sup V. We hit good!" he smiled and looked to their shared mother for approval, before saying any more.

"Mmhm, here girl," Sheronda huffed and handed over a stack of bills. Her share from the various scams they ran from the info she collected from the party.

"Five racks?" she quickly counted and twisted her lips. Kirby averted his eyes when she looked over to him. It was proof that it should have been more.

"Bitch if you brang yo ass 'round 'mo 'offen it 'coulda been 'mo!" she shot back. "Shoot, I ain't no bank! I spend, not hold!"

"You right mama. Them classes be taking all my time!" Vonda apologized. Not because she was wrong, she just didn't want to argue or fight. She sealed the deal and hugged her neck.

"Mmhm," Sheronda hummed and twisted her lips. She felt the love but just didn't know how to love back. Not aborting these six like the six other pregnancies she had aborted was plenty of love as far as she knew. It's just fucked up that loveless people go on to raise more loveless people. Vonda was determined to break all these cycles.

"How's granny?" Vonda asked as she began to summon the Uber. She shook it off when she saw the price and pulled out the card the driver gave her.

"Bout the same," her mother replied and sighed since it was neither good nor bad. The same was better than worse so she smiled.

"I'll walk you out," Kirby offered and fell out the door behind her. Vonda hoped he would and turned.

"What you find out 'bout them niggas?" she asked with a mouthful of malice.

"Everything!" he laughed and handed over the info on the two date rapist as well as the phone she gave him.

Kelondra wanted to put it out of her mind but Vonda had been a victim and wouldn't let it go. One of her mama's many men molested her when she was little. He may have gotten away with it but these two were going to pay.

"Robert McGill and Steven Mullen," she read off the papers with their pictures and info. "Welcome to my wrath!"

CHAPTER FOUR

"I got it!" Vonda declared and rushed to get her money out before Kelondra could pay for it. She started off with the intention of milking her like a spotted cow but now they were friends. It felt good to keep up her share of the friendship and pay for meals sometimes.

"Um, ok. Thanks," Kelondra said and put her card away. She did wonder why her friend always used cash instead of the credit and debit cards she favored. It wouldn't be polite to ask so she would just keep wondering. Her new friend certainly left a lot to wonder about but, friends stay out of friends business.

"Party at Phi-kappa-frappa!" a student announced as he passed out flyers. He put one on the table since neither girl took it from his hand. They both looked down at the party people on the flier then back at each other. They hadn't been to a party since the first one went so wrong. Vonda wanted to go but assumed Kelondra wouldn't while Kelondra assumed the same.

"Looks fun?" Kelondra offered as bait.

"Let's go!" Vonda said, snapping the bait like a hungry catfish does a chicken gizzard. They both had a slew of new clothes in need of an event. The Phi-kappa-frappa party was as good as any.

The besties went back to their dorm-apartment and retreated to their rooms. Once again they weren't competing with each other but they weren't going to be outdone either. They could dress to nines and make the other girls look like mutts though, so that's what they did.

"Killing them hoes!" Vonda declared to her stunning reflection. She was killing it in the mid thigh sundress and sandals but one of them white girls with sweatpants and a T-shirt with a reputation for giving head would still get more play than the both of them.

"Yup!" Kelondra confirmed to her reflection in her own mirror. She was satisfied with how she looked so she stepped out to wait for her friend. She wouldn't have to wait long since Vonda was coming out of her room as well. They both paused and looked at the other in designer sundresses and laughed. "Great minds think alike!"

"And bad bitches dress alike as well!" she cosigned and off they went.

The Phi-kappa-frappa house had been shut down after a rash of overdoses and date rapes but their parties still lived on. They rented a mansion in Buckhead for the night's festivities. Their deposit would most likely be forfeited since they would likely trash the place.

As usual the place was packed with predators.

"We need an Asian for the trifecta!" Steven Mullen sighed. It really was a contest to have every race and demographic represented so they could launch their website on the dark web. Sick dudes would pay good money to watch sleeping and inebriated women being violated.

"Few more black girls too," Robert McGill added. He still missed the one that got away. If he closed his eyes he could still taste Kelondra's sweet box on the tip of his tongue.

"Yeah," his friend sighed since they sure had their share of white girls. Most of their victims voluntarily drank themselves into a stupor and got molested. They woke up sore and sticky and wrote it off as a right of passage.

The monsters were on the hunt and had no idea they were being hunted as well. Vonda knew they were leaders of the frat which was why she jumped at the opportunity. The entire block was bustling with activity when they arrived.

"Glad we didn't drive!" Kelondra said thankfully when they pulled up. On cue a car came through and sideswiped a few cars parked along the crowded street. A blonde head popped up from the driver's lap to explain why he was so distracted.

"Good thing ole Melvin is always on call!" the driver cheered since he ear hustled from the front seat. Vonda used him a few times a week since he drove her to her mother's house.

"Thanks," she said and slid a twenty up front. Kelondra had no choice but to let her pay since the man didn't take credit or debit cards for his wallet.

"Just call when you're ready," he said and watched both booties jiggle under the sundresses. Which is why men love sundresses so much.

The girls joined the throngs of people heading into the party. The front room was a haze of mixed smoke from weed, bongs, cigarettes and hookahs. Electro pop pulsed along with

the strobing lights that gave flashes of happy faces. Only
every face wasn't happy to see them walk in.

"Is that that bitch?" Steven when he spotted the two. The
two brown girls weren't hard to spot in the sea of majority
white faces. There were roughly twice as many Caucasians
than colored which matched the demographics of the
campus.

"Yup, that's that bitch!" Robert moaned and licked his
lips. This time he did close his eyes and savor the flavor in his
mind.

"Fuck this, I'm getting my phone back!" he decided and
marched down the stairs. He twisted and writhed his way
through the crowd and caught up with them at the punch
bowl.

"Have some?" Kelondra asked as she ladled a cup for
herself. She filled the red plastic cup to the rim and took
a sip.

"Are you serious!" Vonda shrieked. She couldn't believe
she was about to drink again after nearly being raped the last
time.

"Serious about just drinking one cup!" she nodded. It was
the fourth cup that had her so fucked up at the last party.
She planned to stick to just one cup tonight. Not that it
mattered much since one cup had as much alcohol as four
cups.

"A'ight," Vonda shrugged. She had done her duty but
wouldn't babysit the girl. She turned away and saw Steven
approach. Her mind said, 'action!' and she got to acting, "Hey
you! I've been looking for you!"

"You have?" he asked, disarmed by her smile.

"Of course, Steven. We got off on the wrong foot," she offered along with his phone.

"Thanks?" he wondered since he wasn't quite sure what just happened. He did know there was a lot of incriminating evidence on the phone so he was happy to have it back. He looked it over and it looked fine even though Kirby was easily able to get inside of it to do what he needed to do. Despite all the security hoops he set up to protect the stash.

"And there she goes..." Vonda laughed as Kelondra hit the dance floor. She laughed, drank and danced while Steven shot his shot. Most barely registered since she was keeping an eye on Robert as well. He was busy pouring a drunk girl another drink. Something Steven said caught her attention and whipped her head in his direction. "Excuse me!"

"I said, you ever let a white guy eat you out?" he asked again.

"Um, no?" she admitted since no guy of any race had ever eaten her out. Curiosity took her by the hand and led her up the stairs. Her brand new vagina was bubbling as they ascended the stairs. Steven and Robert reserved one of the bedrooms for their antics so it was empty when they entered. "Um, keep your lil phone in yo pocket!"

"No problem!" he declared and dipped under the sundress. He pulled her panties aside and dove tongue first into her box.

"Dang!" Vonda declared when she felt his tongue swirl around her labia. A first since her sexual experience was limited to making out a few times, with a few guys. Her back arched completely off the bed when he found her love button. Her whole body writhed in the air as he flicked his tongue up, down and around. "I'm finna cu... Argh!"

"Mmhm," Steven laughed as much as one can laugh with their tongue buried in a bushy box. He had whipped his dick out and rolled a condom on while he ate so he was ready. He rushed up to get inside of her but Vonda had other ideas.

"Un-uh! What you think you're doing!" she fussed and pushed him off of her and the bed.

"I thought, we, I..." he called after her as she marched out of the room.

Vonda found herself blushing and giggled at her first real sexual experience. She bust a good nut in his mouth but was still a virgin. She scanned the party and didn't see her friend. She was almost ready to panic until she saw Robert was working on getting the drunk girl even drunker.

"The hell is this chile at?" she wondered and kept scanning. Her jam came on so she hit the dancefloor and scanned from there. She was late since a handsome guy plucked Kelondra from the dancefloor and took her away.

"In here..." Kelondra's new friend suggested when he pulled the door open to an empty room. She giggled and followed him inside. The one cup was plenty and she was plenty drunk when he whisked her up the stairs and down the hall.

"Mmmm," she moaned when he slid his tongue into her mouth. Then moaned again as he gripped her ass and fondled her breast. But drew the line when he reached her vagina. "No, wait!"

"What? What's wrong?" he asked with the urgency of someone who wants some pussy. He would have slayed a dragon with his bare hands at that moment if it was blocking the box.

"Nothing," she said since explaining she only had sex a few times with Marquis and he was dead was a lot to explain. Instead she lowered herself to his crotch and went for his zipper.

"Oh, ok then," he agreed since a blow job is a nice consolation to some pussy. He looked down and watched as his dick disappeared down her throat. Her soft gags filled the otherwise quiet room. Now it was his turn to moan and groan as he watched and felt the spectacular blow job in motion. A blow job like this can only end one way. Kelondra knew it too and pulled him out of her mouth just in the nic of time. Kelondra finished him off with her hands and he exploded on the homeowners carpet.

"Thanks," Kelondra giggled and left him with his dick out. She had come to have fun and had it. Now she was ready to find her friend so she could go.

"No, thank you," he laughed and tucked his dick away. He stepped back down to the party and came face to face with a familiar face. "Hey you! Vonda, right?"

"Yes!" Vonda cheered, cheesed and nodded. She definitely remembered his name even though they got sidetracked when Kelondra went missing. "Idris!"

"Exactly! And, I'm not letting you get away without getting your number this time!" he insisted and pulled out his phone.

"Six, seven, eight..." she sang and gladly came off the digits. Idris recited his number as well. "I gotta find my friend again. Before she gets in trouble, again."

"No problem. I'll call you tomorrow," he vowed and

leaned down to kiss her cheek. Vonda blushed and giggled until she found her friend back at the punch bowl. "Oh no you don't!"

"I was just looking for you!" Kelondra sang with a slur.

"Girl, I ain't in the bottom of that dang bowl!" she fussed playfully and led her away. Both left the party with a smile courtesy of the same man. One would not remember him while the other couldn't forget him.

CHAPTER FIVE

A pples don't fall far from the tree and Kelondra and her mother were no exception. Madelyn tried to preoccupy her mind with TV but found herself looking instead of watching. Hearing but not listening. The large, empty house seemed to echo her loneliness.

"Fuck this!" she finally decided and marched up to her bedroom. She reached into her nightstand and pulled out her trusty rose. She spun out of her robe and plopped naked on her bed. A good nut would certainly calm her nerves but a flick of the switch only offered more disappointment.

"Oh no!" she wailed at the dead battery. It shouldn't have come as much surprise as much as she had come from the device lately. She reached between her legs to get one the old fashioned way but couldn't seem to find a rhythm. Her lips twisted at the sight of detective Johnson's card in the drawer. She picked it up and twirled it in her fingers, trying to decide if she wanted to call him.

"Mph!" she grunted since he could work wonders with the dick. Still, he was a little creepy and sent a shiver up her spine. He literally solicited her at her son's funeral. She only fucked him to spite her husband. Her face scrunched and she shook off the idea of calling him. Then took it further by balling up his business card and tossing it in the garbage can.

There was a small jazz bar on the outskirts of West View her husband took her to when he was her husband. She remembered him getting quite hot about the attention she was getting from the sax player. He would lock eyes with her and blow his horn like he was playing his horn for her.

He was so jealous he snatched her up out of the club and drug her out to the car. She was shocked he didn't get pulled over as he sped away. But even more shocked when he pulled into an empty parking lot and fucked the daylights out of her. Nothing says 'this is my pussy' better than beating the box up on the side of the street.

That's why Madelyn was headed back to that same bar. That same sax player had just ordered some Uber eats pussy and ain't even know it. And, most pussy is good. New pussy, old pussy, pussy you hadn't hit in a year even reverts back to new pussy. Fat pussy, skinny pussy, tight, loose, it's all good. But unexpected pussy trumps them all. Nothing like some pussy falling into your lap. A windfall of pussy if you will.

"Hmp," she huffed at not having any sort of pain pills in the house. She could go for one right about now to take the edge off. A stiff drink or two would have to do so she made a beeline to the bar as soon as she entered the bar. Madelyn heard the smooth sounds of the sax as she walked through but didn't dare look. She wanted him to see her first and play his horn for her.

"May I help you?" the barkeep asked as she came over.

"Martini with, no. A long island iced tea please," she

decided. She remembered the strong drink from her college days and knew it packed the punch she needed. She even watched her pour the variety of liquors along with a splash of soda to give it the look of ice tea.

Madelyn made a production out of wrapping her full lips around the straw as she turned to face the ensemble belting out a jazz tune. The sax player definitely took notice since he noticed her from the second she walked in since she walked in alone. Especially since most of the sexy women who came in here came with a husband on their arm. In fact, she had the whole attention of the whole band.

It was definitely a love connection for the sax player, except this was a different sax player. Sax players are like rolling stones after all, so the last one rolled away. The last one was a deep chocolate man with a big afro like Shaft. This one was one of those cool white boys with dreads.

"Uh, no," Madelyn told herself and broke off eye contact. The drummer was a hefty three hundred and fifty pounds and the pianist had some Elton John in him.She let out a sigh and shook her head. They could play though, so she listened to song after song until someone came along.

"They're pretty good huh?" a voice asked from her side.

"No!" Madelyn snapped in frustration. The cover band was actually pretty good, they just weren't lay-able and she was trying to get laid. Life got odder when she turned and faced the questioner. "You!"

"Me," Johnson smiled. She did the opposite which made him ask, "What's wrong?"

"You just showed up, out of the blue. That's what's wrong," she fussed.

"And you think..." the detective reeled with slight indignation. "If you think, I'm following you..."

"That's exactly what I think! I don't return your calls and you pop up in the same place I happen to be," she dared.

"The same place I'm at every week! I've been coming here for years. Yet, never seen you here," he defended. Then went there, "For all I know you could be following me!"

"Me! I, follow..." she stammered unsurely. He could very well frequently frequent the place for all she knew. It had been years since her last visit and the place seemed just as popular for the forty and fifty-ish crowd it attracted. "I apologize."

"You should," he huffed and spun on his heels. His mind said 'wait for it' when he lifted his foot to take his first step. It didn't hit the ground before she grabbed his arm.

"I apologized. Let me buy you a drink," she offered from sheer embarrassment. His head began to shake but she wouldn't take his no for an answer. "I insist!"

"Gin and tonic," he reluctantly relented with a sigh as he sat. He noticed the sax player watching and gave him a glare that made him concentrate on his horn.

Johnson nursed his drink while Madelyn guzzled several more of the strong concoctions. The liquor loosened her tongue and she was soon laughing and chatting it up real good. Madelyn had been alone for weeks now and babbled on like a person does when they hadn't spoken to anyone in a while. They gave touches and glances as a prelude to the foreplay to come.

"Mmhm. Is that right? Wow!" he went along with whatever she was saying. Meanwhile he was going over which positions to put her in once they got to their next destination.

She was definitely going in the 'Buck' so he could watch her face as he pounded the bottom of her box for not returning her calls.

"You want to get out of there? Here!" Madelyn suggested in a slur.

"I do," he agreed and stood. She wobbled slightly when she came off the barstool but he was there to catch her. He shot the sax player a wink as they made their way out of the club.

"You should probably drive?" she suggested when she saw her car moving as they came out. It was firmly in place the whole world was spinning.

"Of course," he agreed and led her to his car. He took a mental snapshot of her crotch when he placed her on the passenger seat. The image ended his internal debate on whether or not to eat the pussy. He was definitely going to eat the pussy after getting a glimpse of how plump it was in the white lace panties.

"Are you ok?" Madelyn wondered when he shifted in his seat as he drove her to her house.

"Yeah, it's just..." he said and shifted his erection. There wasn't enough room in his pants for the erection he had. Luckily Madelyn came to the rescue. She reached over and worked it out of his pants. He let out a deep sigh when her hot mouth engulfed him. He hated reaching their destination before reaching his peak but pulled into her driveway.

"Oh? You remembered where I live," she said when she popped up from his lap.

"Of course!" he replied and came around to let her out. He took her keys and opened the door since she was still wobbling. A few minutes later they were on her bed running through the medley of positions he thought about at the bar.

Putting the tracking device on her car had finally paid off.

"AGAIN?" Kirby sighed and tried to mute the sounds of sex coming through the wall. This was the reason he hated having the room that shared a wall with his mother's room. The headboard wall at that. It wasn't bad enough that it was slamming against the wall like a drum beat. No, he could clearly hear the words no male child wants to hear about their mother.

"Damn Sheronda, ssss, you, got, some good, ass, pussy!" Rayford declared with each thrust. Even Kirby knew the end was near when his stroke became choppy.

"Get it! Get it!" Sheronda shouted back and squeezed with perfect timing. She gripped that dick with her strong vagina muscles like a wet gorilla fist.

"Fuck!!" Rayford grunted and let one go. She grabbed his ass cheeks and pulled him to the bottom so he couldn't go anywhere. Not that he wanted to though. The world population increases by the second because someone is busting a nut in someone else every day. Except for maybe Atlanta where so many dudes like dudes.

"That's right daddy! Let it flow," she encouraged and stroked his back like he just stroked her box. Her eyes rolled when she heard the girly giggles of her twins. "Y'all lil heifers get away from my 'doe!"

Panda and Miranda giggled again and scattered before

their mama came out swinging. Sheronda didn't whoop her kids with a belt like normal parents. She would fight them like she would fight some nigga on the street. They got out of there just in time because their mother needed to rush Rayford on his way. He insisted on one for the road which set her behind.

"You still gonna give me that for the rent?" she purred and kissed his face while he dressed.

"You know I got you..." he said and dug into his pocket. He already separated the thousand dollars he promised to give her. It was mainly fives, and tens since he managed a low budget strip club. Actually, The Pussy Trap as the sign said was more a titty bar than a strip club. Sheronda made more from him in a few hours than the girls dancing there made in a whole night of dancing. They made ends meet slinging pussy in the champagne room.

"Thank you baby!" she cheered and kissed him again. She was full of shit most times but was genuinely happy for the money. Especially since her rent was only a hundred bucks after section 8 paid their part.

"You know I got you babe," he vowed. And good pussy will make a man vow to pay rent and utilities. Mediocre pussy may get you a meal, from the drive through.

"Mmhm," Sheronda hummed and twisted her lips when she didn't see her nosey daughters creepy around the hallway. They sat on the steps waiting for their turn to crack for money too. They made a nice little side hustle asking mama's many men for a couple bucks on the way out. They were usually pretty mailable after busting a good nut or three. Plus they didn't want to look bad in front of the mama so they parted with a few bucks. Rayford had that separated as well.

"Hey lil mamas!" he said happily when he saw the girls. They had filled out quite nicely in the year he had been coming around. They may have bodies like their mama but those faces came straight from their ugly daddy. Sheronda's features softened it a bit, but they were still some funny looking girls. Down south the term is 'uglass gals'.

"Hey mister Rayford!" they sang in chorus as he dug into his pocket. He had just parted with their cash when a familiar car pulled into the driveway. The girls were glad they got their money first since they knew it was about to be some trouble. "Uh-oh..."

"What's going on! Who this? Who you homie?" Slim wanted to know as he hopped out of his car and marched across the grass. He directed the question to the twins, then Sheronda, and finally Rayford.

"I'm her nigga!" Rayford declared and stuck his chest out.

"Nigga, I'm her nigga!" Slim shot back and stuck his bird chest out. Never in the history of nigga-dom have niggas been so proud to be niggas. They happily declared their nigga status as Sheronda sat down next to her girls to watch it unfold.

"I got five say slim whoop him," Sheronda bet.

"Un-uh! Mr Rayford don't play!" Panda declared and took that bet. Miranda declined to bet since her mama didn't like to pay. She had plans for the little twenty bucks she just got from Rayford.

"Nigga I'll fight 'fo my love!" Rayford declared and took a swing. Slim watched the wide, looping left as it came in slow motion. He dipped under it and quickly shot off a two piece.

"You finna catch 'deze hands nigga!" he laughed and fired

off a few jabs that popped Rayford in his mouth. The taste of blood set him completely off.

"Aaaaarh..." Rayford growled and scooped Slim off of his feet.

"Uh-oh!" Miranda groaned when he lifted the slender man over his head. She was right too because he slammed him down on his back hard enough to knock the wind out him.

"Dang!" Panda laughed at the puff of dust generated by the impact. The three watched as the two men wrestled in the front yard.

"A'ight y'all, that's enough!" Sheronda finally decided when she grew tired of the wrestling match. The men were men though and still struggled to win. That's why she had to start kicking them both. "I said, that's enough!"

"Dang!" the other twin exclaimed as their mother dominated both men. They didn't understand the power tucked away in their dollar store panties just yet but were getting a hint.

"This ain't none of y'all pussy!" Sheronda declared once she got them separated. "This my pussy! Both of y'all is my niggas! You my nigga, He my nigga! Y'all nigga-in-laws so y'all need to get along!"

"I just broke you off for your rent! I break you off plenty!" Rayford protested.

"I just bought the rent money too?" Slim revealed.

"Yes, but I gotta pay rent err month! What, pay this month and be out on the street next month?" she asked between the two. Her daughters were witnessing a true master at work. "So, unless one of y'all wanna just double up so I on need but one of y'all?"

"Nigga-in-laws..." Slim repeated and nodded at the sound of it. It sure sounded better than giving up twice as much as he was paying already. He looked to Rayford to see how he felt about it.

"I can live with that," the larger man agreed since it wouldn't cost him any more money. He extended his large paw in peace, "Nigga-in-laws."

"Mama don't play!" Panda said in amazement. Not only had the women got the men to shake and share but she coined a new phrase. Nigga-in-laws.

CHAPTER SIX

"Everything is in here!" Steven Mullens reeled when he went through his phone.

"Of course! That nigget can't crack my encryption!" Robert boasted. The incriminating photos and videos were kept in a special folder.

"True that. That nigget had a nice nugget on her!" he declared and licked his lips. They were the only part to touch Vonda's virgin vagina but he lied on his dick. There was no video to confirm or deny so he highly embellished the episode at the party.

"Can't believe you didn't get her on film," his friend declared dubiously. The whole video voyage began to verify his friend's claims. Now it had grown until it crossed the line into date rapes.

"Next time," he said as he checked the incoming files. "What the fuck?"

"What fuck?" Robert laughed and came around to see what pasted a look of disgust on his friend's face. The disgusting images twisted his face as well. "Bro, that's some sick shit!"

"I didn't download this shit!" Steven assured just as the front door came off its hinges.

"Search warrant!" a federal agent shouted and pointed the laser sight of his machine pistol in his face. One move and he would have painted the wall behind him pink with brain matter.

Steve and Robert tried to comply but didn't get a chance. A rush of agents swarmed in and took them down. They were quickly cuffed behind their backs with knees on their necks. Once the suspects were secure the agents began their search. They wouldn't have to look far.

"Looks like we caught them in the act!" the lead agent declared when he picked up the phone from the floor. He had to wince and turn away as if looking at the sun. The images of child porn burned like an arc welder without the mask.

"Sick fuck!" one agent growled and kicked Steven in his head.

"Steven Mullens and Robert McGill, you're under arrest for the possession, manufacturing and distribution of child pornagraphy. You have the right to remain silent..." the agent read while they protested and passed blame.

"We didn't download child porn!" Steven declared while Robert only thought about himself.

"I sure didn't! That's his phone!" he shouted and sold out his friend. "My phone is there! Hold it to my face!"

That was all the consent needed to use the retina scan to open the phone. They followed the instructions from the tip they received and found another trove of child porn.

The other agent came and kicked him in his head too. Because peddlers of child porn should be kicked in their heads. They were hustled out of the dorm amidst the crowd of spectators.

All faces looked shocked when the popular guys were carted out in cuffs. All but Vonda, who knew exactly what was going on. Once Kirby got hold of the phone he was easily able to drop in the spyware that would control the phone remotely.

The back and forth files shared between the two gave Kirby access to Robert's phone as well. Once he loaded them up with enough images to send them away for decades he alerted his sister. She alerted the feds and the two predators were history.

"A DATE!" Kelondra reeled when Vonda relayed her plans for the evening. "With who!"

"This guy. We met at the party," she replied. They actually met at the first party but Vonda was too busy making sure her friend didn't get date raped to get his number.

"I met a guy too..." she sighed and strained to remember his face. It wouldn't come so she tried to recall a name. That didn't register either but she remembered getting freaky with him. The doorbell broke up her train of thought and her friend jumped up to answer.

"Hey!" Vonda cheered when she pulled the door open for her date. She scanned him from his custom Jordan's, expensive jeans and button down shirt.

"Hey yourself!" he replied just as enthusiastically when

he took in the cute dress and sandals she wore. She stepped aside so he could enter and he froze. "I..."

"Are you ok?" Vonda had to wonder when he seemed shocked by her roommate.

"Huh, um..." Idris stammered in search of an excuse. The friendly smile on Kelondra's face gave a hint that she didn't remember him at all. His dick smelled like alcohol after the blow job so it made sense. "Sure, everything is great. I'm Idris."

"Kelondra," Kelondra introduced. This is why it's a good idea to get a name before sucking a dick. She was young and impressionable so there were more nameless dicks in her future. Vonda smiled as her new friend greeted her old friend.

"Are you ready to go?" he turned and asked.

"Yup!" she shot back eagerly since this was the first date she had ever been on. Idris was just as eager since birds of a feather generally flock together. If her roommate was a freak, she probably was too. Little did he know one was a virgin and the other just adventurous.

The next few hours were filled with more first for the somewhat sheltered ghetto girl. She had been in a restaurant that had seats but you had to stand in line and wait for the food. This was the first time an actual waitress brought the food to the table. The first time she had dessert that didn't come out of a cup or container.

"Mmm, this is good!" Vonda declared when she tasted her very first chocolate mousse. She wanted to ask why they called their chocolate pudding a mousse but didn't want to seem ghetto.

"I bet it is!" Idris said seductively enough to make her

wonder if he meant it or her. Meanwhile he was sizing her up for various positions. Her long legs made her an excellent candidate for the infamous 'Buck'. He would put her ankles by his ears and dig her out real good.

"Can I get you anything else?" the waitress asked as she returned. Idris looked at his plate before answering. Her head shook so he spoke up.

"No thank you," he replied and she produced the check. He watched Vonda's eye roam over to the check, then went wide when she saw the amount. The two hundred dollar tab was first followed by another when he wrote in a thirty dollar tip before paying with his credit card.

"Dang!" escaped her mouth before he could stop it.

"You're worth every penny," he quickly shot back. The smile that followed was from her taking it the wrong way. She thought it was a compliment but he was insinuating that he just paid for the pussy.

"I'm stuffed!" Vonda admitted when they headed back out to his car.

'You about to be stuffed for real' Idris mused to his own amusement. The resulting smile made Vonda smile as well. Once again he took it the wrong way. "I need to stop by my place, real quick..."

"Ok," she agreed as he let her into the car. That was her first mistake of the night. The second came when she blushed when he stole a glance between her legs when she sat down.

Idris came from money so he could afford the high rent of the high rise he pulled up to. There was short term parking out front but he pulled into his assigned parking spot since he planned to be in for the night. She smiled when he took her by the hand since it too was a first. As many guys who tried to fuck her since puberty but none of them ever held her hand.

"This is me..." he announced when they reached his unit. He opened the door and stepped aside so she would be awed by the swank apartment.

"Dang!" she declared, like he knew she would. Which is why he liked them young and hood. They were more susceptible to being impressed. Vonda was impressed but not enough for what he had in mind.

"You have to see the stars in my bedroom!" he gushed with such enthusiasm he sucked her in as well.

"Ok!" third mistake as he pulled her into his bedroom. It was well lit when they entered but he quickly hit the lights and shoved her on his bed. "Bruh what the..."

"Hush, just let it happen!" he urged with the sense of urgency that comes with a hard dick. She tried to protest but he shoved his thick tongue into her mouth like a gag.

"Mhhpwfg!" she complained but his tongue in her mouth muffled it into sounds. She now saw the stars he was talking about. They twinkling on his ceiling as he freed his dick from his pants. He began to pull her panties aside and it dawned on her that she was about to be raped.

The tip of his dick touched her labia and gave her new found strength. She summoned everything she had and some more she didn't know she had. It was the strength of her ancestors that helped her shove the man so hard he flipped completely off of his bed.

"Bitch!" Idris fussed and hopped to his feet. Not before the ghetto girl used her ghetto speed and leapt from the bed all the way to the doorway. She had been chased by security guards loaded with merchandise but ran even faster to keep her hymen and dignity intact. The front door brought her to a stop since it was locked. He grabbed her when she tried to unlock the locks. "Un-uh!"

Vonda felt his brute strength when he slammed her against the door. His one track mind ran directly under her dress. Except this ghetto girl had been fighting her whole life. She only coward to her mother and he wasn't her. She threw a straight jab that popped him right in his mouth.

"Come on nigga!" she shouted as he reeled back from the blow. He touched his hand to his mouth and looked at the blood.

"Raggedy ass, ghetto ass, trashy ass..." he berated as he twisted the locks. He had gone from holding her hostage to wanting her gone expeditiously. Now he snatched the door open and shoved her into the hallway. "Fuck 'outa here!"

"Yo mama a raggedy hoe!" Vonda shouted back as she fell. He slammed the door on her before she could finish. Little did he know she was far from finished. A sinister smile spread on her face. She was going to get some payback, one way or the other.

"WHAT HAPPENED?" Kelondra insisted when Vonda was still moping days later.

"Nothing," she pouted since she blamed herself for ordering all that food and dessert. From what she gathered from her classmates ordering dessert was a consent to fuck.

"He was cute tho. I seen him somewhere before..." Kelondra asked and squinted to remember.

"Probably at the party," Vonda sighed. That's where she met him both times and she was at the same party so it made sense.

"May..." she said with the 'be' on the tip of her tongue but she suddenly remembered having him at the tip of her tongue as well. The roof of her mouth and back of her throat as well. "Oh shit!"

"Are you ok?" her friend laughed at her getting stuck mid sentence. Kelondra could literally talk a mile a minute so getting stuck was rare.

"Who? Oh, yeah. Mmhm!" she nodded and quickly changed the station. "Hungry? Let's go eat!"

"I could eat," Vonda agreed. She wasn't particularly hungry but wasn't turning down a free meal. Their friend-ship had evolved passed taking advantage of her every chance she got but still, she wasn't turning down a free meal.

The girls got cute and headed over to the campus hang out. The S&S Chicken and Waffles was situated between several schools which made it even more popular. The bomb ass food only made it even more popular. Arriving early allowed them to grab a good seat before the place was standing room only.

"He's cute!" Kelondra pointed and smiled at a handsome student. The man winced and rolled his eyes before turning his back on her. "What the..."

"He's gay," Vonda laughed when another man came up and hugged him from behind.

"Go on and get monkey pox then, ole monkey ass nigga," the suburban girl hissed. Her urban slang was getting better by the day which wasn't necessarily a good thing.

"Who are you again?" Vonda laughed. Some days her

friend was more her than she was herself. It was a two way street though since the ghetto girl was refining herself as well. Kelondra taught her class without holding a class. They both secretly mocked and copied each other every chance they got.

CHAPTER SEVEN

"Shay, yo daddy on his way over here," Sheronda called down the hall. She had some sass in her tone but that was just the residue from talking to one of her baby daddies. If asked she wouldn't be able to answer why she was so nasty to men. Somehow, somewhere she learned that women were supposed to be snazzy, jazzy and full of attitude.

"Yay!" her six year old cheered and danced while seven year old David pouted.

"Is my daddy finna come too?" he pleaded. His sister's father came on a regular basis while he could hardly remember his father's face.

"Your damn daddy is too busy sucking dick!" she shot down at him. Venom dripped from her chin at the very mention of the man who left her for a man. He would love to come around more often but she was so nasty and he was too sensitive.

"Mr Erik out here!" Panda and Miranda both sang from the porch. Sheronda wasn't the best mother in a worse mother contest but knew enough to keep her hot in ass daughters in the house. The front porch was as far as they could go.

"Let me see what this nigga talmbout..." Sheronda fussed as she went to confront the man. The kids knew to stay put until the yelling stopped. She stepped over her twins and came down the stairs as Shay's father Erik got out. She saw the McDonald's bag and huffed, "Mmhm!"

"Don't start!" he said and braced himself for the bullshit he knew was coming.

"Don't start? Nigga, how you come over here with one damn happy meal!" she demanded.

"Cuz I only got one kid!" he shot back.

"And I got six! Vonda, Panda, Miranda, Kirby, David and Shay!" she counted off. Vonda may have been away at school but it sounded better to make her case.

"Then you should probably drive to McDonald's and buy them some food! I got one kid, one happy meal!" he shot back.

"What about my other kids!" Sheronda fussed for the sake of those kids and the neighbors. Camera phones were watching and would soon have some footage to upload.

"Man, fuck them kids! They not my responsibility!" he fussed and started world war three.

"Nigga fuck you!" the twins shot back from Sheronda's flanks. Shay was inside screaming for her daddy while David began to cry and wail.

"You know what..." Erik decided and tossed the bag to Sheronda. He turned around and stomped back to his car.

"I know you a hoe!" she yelled after him and threw the bag at his back. Neighborhood dogs snatched it and ran off as he pulled away. Curses and insults followed his car down the street until it was out of sight.

"I want my daddy!" Shay pouted and moaned.

"Yo daddy a hoe! Now shut yo mouth 'fo I give you something to cry 'fo!" she spazzed. Just another day in the life of the ratchet family.

It was no wonder Vonda vowed to never return.

"MR RAYFORD OUTSIDE!" little Shay reported to her older sisters. She knew to let the man in when their mama was home but Sheronda was out and the twins were in charge.

"Mama with Slim," Panda reminded. The two Nigga-in-laws had agreed to split time with each other but sometimes schedules overlapped. She only had one vagina after all.

"She said to let him in..." Miranda replied and held up the text. They both hopped up and went to let the man in. As usual they spoke as one person when they pulled the door open. "Hey Mr Rayford! Mama said she will be right back."

"Ok, hey girls," he greeted and fondled them both with his eyes. The two teens weren't allowed to wear the tiny shorts and halter tops outside but they were inside now and Mr Rayford liked what he saw. "You gals about ripe!"

"Thank you," they sang and stuck their chest out a little more. They had started doing that when they first sprouted breast nubs but now they had caught up with their mother's bra size.

"We gonna come dance at the club when we turn eighteen!" Panda declared. Her sister confirmed with a nod and a, "Mmhm."

"Y'all gals can't dance?" he dared and leaned back for the show that was sure to come. The girls giggled for a second before launching into their routine.

"Mmhm, ok then. Alright," Rayford agreed as they shimmied, shook, twerked, popped and dropped. He leaned back to make room for the erection they just made. If they were in his office like most auditions he would have whipped that guy out. Most auditions at the club ended in back shots across his desk or blow jobs under it.

"Mama home!" Shay announced when Slim pulled into the driveway.

The dance came to a screeching halt since they didn't want to have to fight their mama tonight. They rushed into their room to change clothes as well, since that would cause a fight too. Rayford moved around to adjust the hard dick in his pants. Luckily Sheronda had quite a few bags from her outing to bring in. Everyone had gotten themselves together by the time she and Slim walked through the front door.

"My nigga!" Slim greeted his nigga-in-law when he saw him on the sofa. He put the bags down as Rayford stood.

"My nigga!" Rayford shot back and gave him a pound and man hug while Sheronda just shook her head. "Come by the club later!"

"Sho nuff," Slim agreed and turned to leave. He had dropped a few hundred bucks on Sheronda but got his money's worth. He snickered to himself as he walked out the door, "Bet not kiss her, mouth kinda salty right now..."

"Hey baby!" Sheronda cheered and rushed over for a hug. Rayford couldn't read minds so he stuck his tongue in her salty mouth anyway. She felt the erection and pressed into it. "I see you glad to see me!"

"Mmhm," he lied since it was a leftover erection from her daughters. Which was probably fair since the salty taste in her mouth was leftover nut from Slim.

"You got something for us!" David declared as he and the rest of the kids showed up in the living room. They just knew with all those bags she got something for them.

"Uh no! Y'all ain't paid for none of this!" she declared and scooped her bags up. Rayford had to help out and carry them into her room. He looked back at the twins looking at him as he went to fuck their mama. He fucked their mama alright but it was their faces he saw when he closed his eyes.

"A JOB!" Kelondra reeled as if the word was a snake.

"Uh, yeah. My mama not rich, remember," Vonda reminded as she prepared for her first day at the new job.

"I guess but..." she replied but held her but. She didn't mind spending on her friend but knew her friend had a point.

"Plus it's easy work. Just checking ID at the library," she shrugged.

"Sounds pretty easy," Kelondra huffed and twisted her lips. She had her own dilemma as to what she was going to do by herself. Vonda seemed to sense it too and softened.

"I'll be back in a few hours. Then we can hit that party!" she suggested and her friend eagerly accepted.

"Ok," she relented and let up. She still planned to get out while her friend went to work.

Vonda had ulterior motives for the job. The fifteen bucks an hour was good for a freshman but she planned to make a lot more than that. Once she clocked in and took over the entry desk she got down to work. She propped her phone up where the camera lens could catch everything. Then used a second phone to make a call.

"Hey. It's perfect!" Kirby declared when he took the call. The video from the other phone was crystal clear. The test of their plan came a second later.

"ID please," Vonda asked and smiled at the student who arrived. The girl quickly complied and flipped her wallet open. "Social security card as well, please."

"When did they start this?" the student wondered as she flipped to that as well.

"Just recently. Just need to verify the name," she said, barely looking at the card. Which put the student at ease since she didn't like the extra measures. Most didn't but Vonda made a big show of not looking when they produced the extra identification. She didn't need to look since Kirby was across town recording names, date of birth and social security numbers.

"Well, well, well..." a familiar face smiled as it approached.

"ID and social!" Vonda huffed and turned her head away from the man who kicked her out of his apartment.

"Social?" he wondered like everyone else but complied like the rest of them when she didn't answer. "So, you work here?"

"No, I work here!" she shot back sarcastically and looked to the line behind him.

"You know what..." he decided and spun on his heels. Vonda twisted her lips and grabbed her phone.

"Yo," Kirby answered.

"Tell me you got that last one!" she urged as she let the next people in line inside without checking.

"Idris Lyapo. Born December..." he said and rattled off his info. A smile grew wider with each word. Same for Idris who's smile grew wider with each step.

"WHO IS IT?" Kelondra wondered when she heard the doorbell sing its song. Her only friend had only been gone an hour which meant she had three more hours to be alone. She pulled the door open and tilted her head at the caller.

"Something tells me you remember me now?" he asked as he invited himself in.

"Um, I mean, we," she stammered. "Vonda is at work."

"I know. I just saw her. That's why I'm here," he said and walked up on top of her. "To return the favor..."

"I, we, she," Kelondra stammered some more but was no match for his seduction and her inner freak. He shut her up by sliding his tongue into her mouth.

Kelondra moaned and her knees buckled beneath her. Luckily Idris was there to catch her. He scooped her up and carried her to the sofa. She could only watch as he pulled her shorts and panties off. Then kneeled like she was the queen.

Kelondra gave her consent by lifting one leg on the back of the sofa. Her luscious vagina bloomed and blossomed like a spring flower. A puddle of honey dew formed from the anticipation. He returned the favor indeed when he leaned in and sucked it up.

"Awe man!" Kelondra protested when his tongue began to twirl. Her lovely labia hadn't been licked since she and Carey had first gotten together. They would trade oral sex to satisfy their lust while saving her virginity. She just gripped the throw pillows when he concentrated his suction on her clitoris. That did the trick and sent shivers up her spine.

He got what he came for when she came in his mouth. They locked eyes for a moment to figure out what was next. He wouldn't mind another round in her mouth but her box was literally bubbling on his fingers. He slid one inside while they stared at each other.

"Go ahead," she nodded and pulled that leg down. She was ready to give him some pussy, just not that much pussy.

He quickly wrapped his wood in some rubber and rubbed it against her slippery box. He looked curiously when it took more pressure to enter than the average box. Most of their classmates were fucking enough to fall to the bottom with little effort.

"I'm sorry," Kelondra offered when she saw him grimace.

"Don't be..." he replied since tight pussy is nothing to be sorry about. He kissed her lips as he eased his way inside. Now it was her turn to grimace as he filled her up. She regretted going this far but felt it was too far to turn back. Katie had told her that once she made a guy hard it was an obligation to make him soft again. She contemplated asking him to stop, so she could return the favor he just returned. She spent more time thinking than she actually had and that good, vice-like vagina got the best of him. "Shit!"

"I'm sorry," she repeated when Idris looked like he was in

pain. And sometimes a good nut is excruciatingly pleasurable enough to look like pain.

"Don't be," he repeated and pumped the latex full of little swimmers. As much as he hated he withdrew the dick and stood.

"There..." she said, pointing to her bedroom where her bathroom was. Kelondra watched him waddle into her room with his pants down before pulling her own panties and shorts back up. She twisted her lips and shook her head at her own temerity. She usually could blame the alcohol or weed for rash decisions, but she was stone cold sober at the moment. "I need a drink."

"What's that?" Idris asked, fresh from washing his dick in her sink.

"Huh? Oh, nothing. Vonda will be home from work soon," she said and stood to let him out.

"When will she be back at work?" is what he wanted to know when he pulled her into an embrace. Her plan was to reject him and send him on his way until she felt the comfort of his arms wrapped around her.

"I'll find out, and let you know," she purred, powerless to stop the words from coming. It was like her vagina spoke through her mouth like a ventriloquist.

"Do that," he ordered and kissed her again. He felt her knees buckle again but there was no time for round two. Kelondra was stuck in the same place for several minutes after he left. Only her phone buzzing on the table snapped her from her daze.

"Um, hey," she answered.

"What's wrong with you?" Vonda asked immediately when she heard the guilt coming through the line.

"Who? Oh, nah," Kelondra shot back like it made sense.

"Anyway, get dressed. We finna hit this party!" her room-mate cheered.

"I thought you didn't get off for another hour?" she asked and checked her watch. The front door began to open making her wonder if Idris had come back for another round.

"Girl, that job..." Vonda was saying as she came in. They were face to face so she lowered the phone and finished her statement. "Ain't me!"

"You just came home?" Kelondra shrieked. She just knew she had to pass Idris in the hall but only for the daze he left her in twenty minutes ago.

"Uh, yeah. And I'm tryna get back out the 'doe. So get dressed!" Vonda fussed playfully. The busy library proved to be a gold mine. She had collected information on a couple hundred students since she arrived. Which gave her no reasons to stay. They would make a hundred times what the job could pay just off one identity.

"Ok! I'm coming!" Kelondra sighed and regretted it. She got guilty again since she did just come in Idris's mouth a few feet away.

"Such an odd girl," Vonda chuckled at the range of emotions that just ran across her face. She shook her own head and headed in her room to shower and change.

CHAPTER EIGHT

"We need to talk!" Vonda announced as she came into the apartment.

"I know," Kelondra sighed and mentally prepared. She knew this day would come since she and Idris had been seeing each other anytime she had a free moment. "I really didn't mean for this to happen. It's just..."

"Girl, what the hell are you talking about?" Vonda laughed.

"Huh? Oh! Nothing," she laughed and played it off when she realized she wasn't caught, yet. "What's up?"

"I'm talking about this party Friday," she explained and held up the flier. "Now, what are you talking about?"

"Who? Oh, same," Kelondra laughed. She could always get out of a jam by acting dingy. Vonda caught on since they were both learning from the other.

"Anyway, let's go shopping!" Vonda offered as her phone buzzed. Her face changed when she saw the name on the screen and took the call. She rushed to her room to take the call in private. "Hey mama."

"Don't hey mama me! Where my cut? And don't lie, yo brother told me all about it!" Sheronda growled. She was still holding Kirby by his ear and gave it a twist.

"Owwwwe!" her brother moaned. "Just tell her!"

"Yeah, we ran some numbers but, that's our lick," she protested and stuck her chest out since her mother couldn't see.

"First of all..." Sheronda began. When she started like that it meant a lot was to follow. "Ain't no, 'our lick!'. Err lick I hit go to take care of y'all! And second, I know you got ya lil chest poked out!"

"No I don't," she moaned and shrank. Sheronda hit plenty of licks but didn't cut her in so why should she have to cut her in. Plus, she didn't even live there any more so why should she cut her in. She had more valid points but kept them all to herself. "We still got more numbers to work. We'll cut you in..."

"Y'all ain't finna cut me in shit! I'm taking the rest of them numbers. I might, might cut you two in!" Sheronda said and hung up.

"Shit!" Vonda fussed at her bad luck. She already knew her mother had her brother in a headlock, making him give up the numbers she got from the library. They could have worked them for months but her reckless mother would squander them in weeks.

"What's wrong?" Kelondra asked as she came to the rescue. Vonda was too distraught for words so she just sobbed. When her friend scooped her up it only made her cry harder. Hard enough to reveal her hustle.

"I'm a scammer. My whole family is," Vonda blurted. She was amazed at how good the truth felt on her tongue so she went for more. "That library job was just a hustle to get numbers."

"Numbers?" Kelondra cut in so she could follow along better.

"Dates of birth, social security. Identities ain't nothing but numbers. Once we get the numbers we own the identity. My little brother is a genius but my mama keep her knee in his neck," she explained.

"Ouch," she reeled at the painful reference. Then cheered back up when she got an idea. "Ooh! Ooh!"

"What?" Vonda laughed. Her friend's goofy laugh always made her feel better.

"I know a guy! Turbo! He went to high school with us!" she recalled. The super nerd was known for schemes and scams since ninth grade.

"But she took all my numbers!" Vonda added to see if she had a solution for that as well. Kelondra bit the inside of her cheek as she pondered that dilemma. A smile spread on her face when a solution came to mind. "What?"

"I just saw a sign for help wanted in the registrar's office!" she remembered. Only because she was checking the student board for the next party.

"Ion think they finna give me 'nare 'nother job," Vonda stated correctly since she walked out on the last job.

"I'll get it!" Kelondra offered before even checking with herself. The excitement of doing something illegal was all the approval she needed. "Hell yeah!"

"We need to go see this Turbo guy asap!" Vonda declared.

"Except, his sister cheated with my ex," she snarled at the

thought of Roslyn. Her face scrunched at the memory of the videos that surfaced from her time in the hood.

"That's bad!" Vonda laughed at her reaction. She still didn't intend to let whatever it was stand in the way of her money. "Well, she can have that nigga!"

"Oh, he's dead," she recalled even though she missed Carey Junior's funeral. The once popular, athlete only had two people see him off. They only came since he was their son.

"Well, let's go see this, Turbo!"

TURBO WASN'T hard to find since he was still in West view. He was now a senior with scholarship offers from coast to coast. Still in the basement, happily hacking into systems just to prove that he could. He jumped at the chance to meet Kelondra and rushed down town.

"I bet that's him!" Vonda laughed at the gangly, white teen as he entered. He leaned his head back to ke
ep the coke bottle glasses on his long, angular nose.

"You'd win that bet," Kelondra laughed and stood to waive him over to their table.

"Hey Kelondra!" Turbo cheered and threw his arms wide for a hug but got mushed instead.

"As if!" she laughed as she pushed his face away. Once they sat she made the introduction and her pitch. "This is my friend Vonda. How would you like to make some money?"

"Like C-note and Keto?" he literally reeled back in his chair. The murders would be a deterrent to drug dealing until the freshman became seniors. Most had sworn off the thug life and enjoyed the suburbs and life. Especially his sister who still had a sore throat from her foray into the dark side.

"A what?" Vonda looked to Kelondra who just shook it off.

"Not like that. White collar stuff," she replied and turned it back over to Vonda.

"We can get identities. Can you get accounts?" she dared.

"Can I get accounts? Can I, turbo, get accounts!" he bragged just like she hoped he would. Kirby was king when he came to running scams and had the same cocky attitude. "Not only can I get accounts, I can get credit cards, identification cards, car notes..."

"He's our guy!" Vonda declared.

"Maybe..." Kelondra said and paused for attention. "Don't tell your sister!"

"What sister?" Turbo wanted to know as he looked between the two women.

"Yup, he's our guy," Kelondra cosigned. Now it was her job to get the numbers from the registrar's office. That job proved even easier than she thought since turbo provided her with a thumb drive. Once she inserted it into the computer at work the hacker had access to the whole database. Not just current students but records going back ten years. The scammers had just struck gold.

"SO, can we just use these credit cards? Like we're them?" Kelondra wanted to know. The rush of excitement was almost sexual since she and Idris were still sneaking around.

It gave her the same tingly feeling in her panties as his smile did.

"We are them!" Vonda laughed and produced a driver's license with Kelondra's face but another students' info. Turbo started slow and only worked the identities that didn't have active credit. They were good for five thousand dollar credit limits.

"So I'm Contessa Freeman?" she asked as she looked at the ID.

"And I'm Mandy MacArthur. So let's go shopping!" Vonda cheered. Giving these two girls the power to shop was like giving a loaded gun to a lonely white teenage boy. It was bound to be a problem.

Online shopping is the best way to pull off scams if one has an address to ship to. Sending stolen goods to where you live is the same as ordering some police like door dash. Shopping in person has its dangers too but Vonda was a vet. Sheronda had groomed her since a child so they wore wigs and glasses since they would be on camera.

By the end of the day they had burned through the credit limits Turbo had set up. They made sure to pick up the hardware and software he requested as his cut. Once they started using the identities with established credit they could start getting cash and cars. That's when the real

money would come.

"Wow! Just eff-ing wow!" Kelondra proclaimed when she looked at all of the merchandise on her bed. She could easily and certainly gotten it between her parents but getting it on her own was kinda sweet. Not to mention the thrill of doing something illegal gave her the same feeling as Idris did when licking between her legs. The sex was more intense just from the sneaking around her roommate.

"Once again the hottest chicks in the party!" Vonda agreed. She had an array of designer labels laid out as well. Including some for her twin sisters at home. Trick was getting it to them without their mother finding out.

They retreated to their bedrooms to change and reconvened a half hour later. Both admired the other's outfit and headed out. Tonight's party was held at another frat house packed to the gills. It had spilled out into the front and back yards by the time they arrived.

"Dang!" they both exclaimed as one since they were becoming one personality. The crowd around the dance floor meant someone was putting on so they squeezed in for a look.

"Dang!" Kelondra said alone this time at the two girls twerking up a storm on the floor while the crowd tossed money. Vonda didn't join this 'dang' since she knew the girls.

"Oh hell naw!" she fussed and shoved her way forward to a chorus of gripes and complaints. They grew even louder when she snatched the twerkers up and out the back door. The two girls scrambled to scrape up their money before she could.

"What you doing!" Panda protested, while Miranda nodded.

"What am I doing? What the fuck are y'all doing!" she barked at the twins. Another question came to mind so she added that one as well. "What are y'all even doing here!"

"Trying to get paid!" Miranda shouted back, while her sister added her part. "Mama don't give us shit!"

"A'ight now," Vonda warned but her sisters didn't back

down like they would before. She used to whoop them both when they were younger but they were as big as she was now. Plus there were two of them that thought and moved as one.

"A'ight now what?" Panda asked as if it were a strain. "You not our mama."

"For real. We the same age as you!" the other twin reminded since the three were Irish twins nearly ten months apart. They were technically in the twelfth grade but skipped too much school to hope to graduate. Plus, they were both pretty dumb like their daddy.

"You right," Vonda said and raised her hands. "I'm just tryna look out for y'all. Since y'all mama sure ain't!"

"You right sis. We just tryna make some bread," Miranda explained. Vonda knew all too well their mother was all for herself.

"I know. I got y'all some clothes at my spot. Let's have some fun and turn up!" she relented and looked around for her roommate. Her head shook when she found her exactly where she knew she would. "Whatever y'all do, don't drink none of that punch!"

Kelondra got pissy drunk once again and once again had to be saved from herself. Vonda plucked her away from a group of men before they could cart her away and run a train. The twins helped Vonda get her into the car at the end of the night to take them home.

CHAPTER NINE

"Dang!" Panda and Miranda announced when they entered the apartment for the first time. Had it not been for the party she may not have ever invited them over. First, because they were ratchet as fuck. Plus, they had sticky fingers.

"Ooh, I wanna go to college too now!" Miranda gushed as they looked around. "Dey 'ga y'all 'di 'partment?"

"Uh, first of all, you gotta finish high school!" Vonda reminded and shook her head at the clipped words. It was hard to believe she used to speak 'li 'tha, not too long ago. "And, yo lil ass don't like to go!"

"If they let us smoke weed in class we be there err day!" Panda cheered and got a high five from her lookalike, think alike sister.

Her older sister could only shake her head. They were on different planets for them to have grown up in the same house. Vonda may have been just as ratchet as them once upon a time, but wanted out of the hood. She knew school was her way and buckled down to get through it. Her efforts paid off when she won the full ride scholarship. She vowed to never go back. She left her sisters in the living room to look around while she put Kelondra to bed.

"Yo phone ranging girl," Vonda teased as she helped Kelondra out of her clothes. She did a double take at the name on the screen and scrunched her face. Curiosity got the best of her so she took the call. "Hello?"

"Kelondra?" Idris asked when he didn't recognize the voice. Vonda opened her mouth to curse him out but quickly remembered she had no right to. She had no rights to the man she didn't want and couldn't be mad. At least not at him. She twisted her lips at Kelondra and accepted that maybe they weren't as close as she thought they were. Then remembered she couldn't be mad at her for wanting a man she didn't want. She felt something, just not sure what it was.

"Look! Look! Look," the twins exclaimed as they took turns pointing around the room and again at the view. They looked and saw their sister return with a confused look on her face. "What's wrong?"

"Huh? Oh, nothing. Come on..." she said and directed them to her room. The clothes she bought for them were laid out on the bed.

"Dang!" they sang, danced and twerked in celebration. For some odd reason ghetto girls twerk when happy. The twins filled their big sister in on most of the goings on in the house. Her head shook until it began to get heavy from the long day. The twins watched their big sister yawn, blink, then curl up on her bed and begin to snore.

The two twins technically had two brains but they thought as one. Both silently stood and began looking around the room. Panda found a few loose dollars and tucked them into her pocket. Miranda looked at her sister's jewelry but shook the thought from her head. They learned from experience that stealing too much could be more problems than it was worth. There are acceptable losses people will take. Going beyond that could be dangerous.

Both had the same thought at the same time and crept out of the room. They followed each other's lead that led them right to Kelondra's door. Her drunken snores were an invitation so they crept inside. Both were semi-professional thieves so they got straight to work. Panda went straight for the clothes hamper since those clothes would take longer to be missed. Someone is quicker to miss something they intend to wear versus something they already wore.

She held up a pair of the rich girl's expensive panties and gave them a sniff. They smelled like they hadn't been worn since Kelondra kept a well maintained vagina. Next came the matching bra and Miranda nodded in approval. She rummaged around and collected all the panties and bras from the bin. Meanwhile Miranda pilfered her purse for change and loose bills. Panda looked curiously at the various credit cards and matching ID cards on the dresser. Sheronda let them pickpocket and boost but never let them in on the credit card hustle. That's exactly why she plucked one of each.

They took their haul and crept back over to their sister's room and hid the loot in with the clothes Vonda bought for them. The twins huddled on the pallet they made and slid into sleep themselves.

"YOU SURE YOU don't want me to drive you guys?"
Kelondra asked when Vonda summoned Melvin to take her
sisters home.

"Hells yeah!" the two twins cheered as one. If they would
just put their half brains together it might be enough to think
straight. They knew they would get props from their poor
peers from being seen in the fancy car.

"We good," Vonda sighed and declined. She twisted her
lips at having to deal with her mother herself and certainly
didn't want to subject her friend to Sheronda's antics. She
twisted her lips to the other side when she looked at the bags
her sisters carried. They looked bigger than they did last
night but she shrugged it off since the car had arrived.

Kelondra pouted as they walked out and left her alone.
She was fronting tho because she shot Idris a picture of her
vagina as an invitation to come fill it up. He jumped at the
offer and rushed over and inside of her. They both got a good
nut before Vonda and the twins made it to the house.

"Panda and Miranda home!" David shouted when he saw
his sisters pull up. He knew they were in trouble for staying
out all night. Seeing Vonda get out behind them made the
boy squeal and run over. "Vonda!"

"Hey lil boy," Vonda laughed as her brother hugged and
loved on her. She hated leaving them with their mother as
much as she loved being away from their mother. The same
mother who appeared at the door with hands on hip.

"Mmhm, y'all lil heifers grown now huh?" she dared. All
eyes shot down to her feet. If she had on her house shoes she
would more likely just talk shit and make threats. She had on
her tennis shoes today which meant she was ready to fight.

"They spent the night with me," Vonda offered in their

defense. She extended the Gucci shopping bag out as an offering.

"They bags bigger than mine?" the ungrateful mother wondered.

"But yours is Gucci, they just got clothes," Vonda explained.

"Mmhm..." Sheronda hummed and pulled the handbag from the shopping bag. She looked at the four hundred dollar price tag and twisted her lips. "Shoot you 'coulda just gave me the four 'huned! I 'woulda got me one for thirty and had me two 'huned 'leff over!"

"My bad mama," she said, ignoring the bad math. The twins didn't catch it since they were just as dumb. Instead they snickered at the reprieve and rushed into their bedroom before their mother could tax them too. She encouraged them to steal and scam as long as she got her cut.

"So, why you ain't never invite me to your 'partment?" Sheronda wanted to know.

"Huh?" she asked, meaning never. The pause gave her time to come up with an excuse. "Yeah cuz I had to sneak them in after the party."

"So when you gonna invite me to the party?" she dared and cocked her head.

"Huh? Oh, next one," she lied and checked her phone. She read the imaginary message out loud, "My ride ready."

"A'ight," Sheronda dared and cocked her head to the other side. She intended to hold her to her words too. As soon as she walked out she called for the twins. "Y'all heifers come here and let me see what y'all got!"

"Shoot!" Panda fussed at not separating the new clothes

before her mother saw them. They both pouted as they went back out to pay their taxes.

"Mmhm..." Sheronda hummed as she dumped Miranda's bag out on the sofa. "Girl these the good drawers! Y'all fine with dolla sto panties!"

"Awe man!" Panda protested as they both lost the first matching bra and panty sets of their lives. Sheronda was naked under her robe so she pulled a pair on right then. The twins snickered knowing they came from a hamper. Luckily Kelondra took good care of her vagina.

"At least she ain't get this!" Miranda cheesed at the credit card and ID she lifted from Kelondra who just so happened to be looking for it at the moment.

"COME ON WITH THEM CARDS. Let's dispose of it properly so we don't have any mishaps," Vonda reminded.

"Fa sho," Kelondra sang and nodded at how authentic it sounded. She was becoming more Ki-ki than Kelondra by the day. The same way Kenneth transformed into Keto before he was killed. Her lips twisted when the cards weren't exactly where she knew she put them in her purse.

"What's wrong?" her friend asked to match to look on her face.

"I know I..." she was saying as she checked another compartment. It wouldn't have been there since that's where she kept her cash. That wasn't there either which made her frown even deeper.

'Oh Lawd' Vonda thought to herself since her sisters had spent the night. If anything was missing she knew them well enough to know they took it. She left Kelondra to her futile search to make sure none of her stuff was missing. All the twins could do with those cards was get themselves in trouble. It would be good for them if they were stealing in the first place.

"What the fuck?" Kelondra wondered since when something isn't exactly where you know you left it makes one wonder what the fuck.

"What's wrong?" her roommate asked when she returned from checking her room for missing items.

"I can't find, I had that, hmm!" she muttered as she searched her purse. Her face scrunched some more when she didn't see the money she would have sworn she had in the purse as well. Vonda would have known her sticky-fingered sisters would have stolen whatever was missing but Kelondra shrugged it off. Only because she was getting drunk pretty regularly lately.

"Anyway, let's meet with Turbo so we can get some more work!" Vonda suggested. They had to give him his nerd gear they bought for him as well.

"Let's!" Kelondra agreed. They headed across town to meet him to make the swap, so they could go shopping.

Luckily they chose the higher ends malls since the twins were in the low budget mall loading up on low budget clothing and shoes. This proved the old adage was still relevant about a fool and his money soon parting. The residue credit allowed them to get away with it this time. Next time they wouldn't be so lucky.

❄

"KITA, THAT'S THEM," the clerk whispered to her manager as the twins came back to the scene of their crime. They struck pretty good at the Foot Locker last time so they had to come back for more. It was she who let them rock with the credit cards since she got a commission.

"We need to 'hurr up 'fo mama get home with Slim," Miranda said as they looked over the wall of tennis shoes like a MacDonald's menu.

"Girl you know it's Rayford turn!" Panda reminded since Slim went yesterday. The twins saw the same behavior from their mother as their sister had but it had different effects.

Vonda still had a virgin vagina with no intention of parting with any pussy. She was repulsed by the revolving door in and out of her mother's body. The woman had Many Men, many many, many men, like a Fifty Cent song. Panda and Miranda on the other hand were amazed by the power of the P. They were destined to be hoes after watching their mother work her box like a full time job.

Sheronda rarely worked since these tricks were so easy to trick. Women catch all the flack for being hoes but it's solely the men of society's fault. When men went back to being the protectors and maintainers of women like God created them to be then the women could go back to being women.

Unfortunately just having a penis doesn't make a male a man no more than a vagina makes a female a lady. Luckily Sheronda kept a tight rein on her girls since she wasn't ready to be a grandmother at thirty six. She was hoping to hold out until at least forty.

"Mmhm," the manager agreed when she recognized them from the security footage. The store had to eat the cost of the first theft so this time she called the police. "Get them whatever they want."

"You for real?" the clerk asked until she heard her speaking to 9-1-1. This was the hood so she knew they would be a while. "I'll stall them."

"Hey, you got these in a nine?" Panda asked, holding up a pair of pink Air Max.

"Two!" her twin added and held up the latest P-money tennis shoes. "Dese hoes too!"

"We got the jogging pants too!" the clerk suggested and nodded both their heads. Why not get the matching P-money jogging pants since they were all free.

"Come on with them!" they said as one and off she went. Except the clerk went to the rear to turn the camera app on so she could go live.

"I'm finna get some of dese too!" Panda decided which made her twin decide on something else as well. They were so busy adding to their haul they didn't notice the delay. They were well above the felony range by the time they reached the counter. Perfect timing since the police were just walking in as Kita rang up the sale.

"Y'all got ID?" she asked when Panda presented the credit card.

"Mmhm, shole do..." she said and proudly presented it.

"This them..." she said behind them once the crime was officially committed. The twins turned to see the police standing behind them. Once again their half brains were in sync and they both bolted in different directions.

Miranda was always the quicker of the two but she just picked the wrong route. Panda scurried off towards the shoe wall and made a break for the door. Her twin went the other direction and trapped herself off. The cops were overweight and out of shape but this time it worked to their advantage. They didn't have to chase her since she was trapped.

"Fuck! Mama's gonna kill me!" Panda moaned as she watched her sister getting handcuffed. She was right too since Sheronda warned them both to never leave the other, anywhere, ever. Never coming home again was better than coming home alone. There was only one thing she could do so she did it and walked back into the store. "Y'all got us. Just don't call our mama!"

CHAPTER TEN

"Where are they?" the newest addition to the white collar crime division asked as she came into the office.

Latisha Adams and Johnson had both been reassigned after some money came up missing from a murder scene. They both stole it so they couldn't sell the other out. As a result, both got transferred to a less prestigious position. The irony of putting the crooks in direct contact with more financial crimes wasn't lost on them.

They made plenty of arrests and cases on small to mid sized capers. Whenever they came across a big fish they wanted in. They planned to skim and scam their way into retirement. Johnson already purchased a plot of land in the Dominican Republic where he planned to build a villa filled with vagina. He would book sex tourism vacations for fellow fucked up fellows like himself.

"Rooms two and three," the officer said with a smirk.

"What?" she asked curiously.

"You'll see," he replied and went back to work.

"Always something around here..." she sighed and skimmed the report as she walked. A pattern had developed recently involving students from Atlanta Tech students. This was one but being used in the low rent mall was odd enough to get an interview. She walked into room two only because it was closer and ignored the girl sitting across the desk while reading the report. She continued reading while the suspect tried to read her. Her lips twisted dubiously just before her head lifted. "Where'd you get this card?"

"Ion know nothing 'bout nothing!" Panda declared. She crossed her arms over her chest and turned her face to the side. That was clear body language for 'I said what I said', and Latisha accepted it.

"Check," she said and stood. There was still another suspect so she headed out and over to the next room. She walked in and did a double take at the same face she left in the next room. Her face scrunched when she went back into the report. The rhyming names nodded her head and un-scrunched her face. "Twins."

"Ion know..." Miranda began but Latisha beat her to it.

"Nothing 'bout nothing. I know. That's why I ain't finna ask you nothing," she said as she slid into one of her many personas. Good detective work requires good acting skills and she was one of the best. The ghetto girl demeanor instantly resonated with the ghetto girl. "Ain't no snitching shawty!"

"All facts! No caps!" Miranda shot back. Still, Latisha saw through the facade and knew she was the weaker of the two twins.

"Shoot, I'm just gonna write this up that y'all found the card. And tried it out?" she led to see if the girl would follow.

"Mmhm. Shole nuff," Miranda nodded in agreement as Latisha wrote.

"Y'all go to A.T?" she asked offhandedly as she scribbled nothing that had anything to do with anything.

"What's that?" she asked and answered at the same time. Had she attended Atlanta Tech she would certainly know the initials.

"Nothing," she shrugged and tilted her head as she continued to scribble. "Who y'all know who goes to college?"

"My big sister V. Well, Vonda. She goes to Atlanta, um, school. College?" Miranda tried to remember. "We just went to a party there. It was lit!"

"I heard they were popping!" the detective cheered. Not at the college parties but because she now had a lead and something to actually write down, Vonda Perry, a student at Atlanta Tech.

"I KNOW these lil heifers ain't..." Sheronda growled as they rode to the precinct to pick up her offspring.

"Just take it easy. They finna be fine," Rayford soothed and patted her hand. He was going to put up the bond to bail the girls out so they wouldn't have to sit in jail for a year to get to court.

"These hoes have been busting credit cards on they own and ain't even giving me my cut!" she fumed.

Rayford had to turn to look at her to make sure he heard her correctly. Her daughters were in the dangerous county jail and her main concern was her cut. He was glad he just parted with another grand for another abortion since he wouldn't want to have a kid with her. Ironically it wouldn't stop him from fucking her raw or busting in her.

"Yeah, well..." he sighed and pulled into the parking lot. They went inside the jail where the bondsman awaited for his twelve percent of the bail.

"That must be mama bear," Latisha mentioned when he saw Sheronda in the lobby. Her partner peeked up from the porn on his laptop for a peek himself. He first saw the twins from behind and came around to see their faces. Some chicks just look better from the back. Panda and Miranda were some chicks but he wanted to see the mama.

"Oh, ok," Johnson remarked when he saw Sheronda was actually quite pretty. Her daughters got the round asses from her, which led him to surmise. "They must look like their daddy."

"I'm sure cuz..." Latisha was saying until she realized she was saying it to herself because her partner had taken off.

"Mrs Perry? Detective Johnson," Johnson asked and offered as he came up on Sheronda arranging bail for her babies.

"And?" she snarled at him with 'fuck the police' written all over her face.

"And, I can help with your daughter's problem," he replied and extended his card. "That's if you want it."

"Mmhm, and what do you want?" Sheronda asked as she followed his eyes down to her breast, crotch and back up to her breast.

"All that, if you want it," he said and walked away once she took his card. She twisted her lips at the card before tucking it into her purse. The papers were signed and the twins were released.

"Mama, it ain't even like that," Panda explained as they came through the door.

"We found them cards!" Miranda cosigned since the cop told her the same.

"And I found a bunch of new clothes in y'all closet! Tried to hide this shit!" Sheronda said wearing some of the new clothes she found. She had confiscated everything with a tag as penance for their transgressions. "And y'all ain't found shit! Y'all lil heifers finna tell me where y'all got them from?"

The twins looked at each other but Miranda looked more to Panda since she was the leader. They hated to tell on their sister but in the end only cared about themselves. Vonda left them to live in a fancy building with fancy friends who drove fancy cars. She even talked fancy, saying whole words instead of clipping them off at the end like the hood.

"Well!" Sheronda shouted so ferociously even Rayford was startled. The car swerved from the outburst but he maintained his control. Not before Sheronda shook her head at him too. "Let me find out..."

"Vonda gave it to us," Miranda began and let her sister finish. "She be getting a lot of them!"

"I hate a bitch who forgets where they come from," Sheronda growled. "Sometimes you just gotta remind em..."

'I'M HERE' came the text that set Kelondra in motion. She cut her TV and listened from her door. Hearing nothing, she crept out and tiptoed across the living room. The plush carpet helped her cause and muffled her steps.

Kelondra let out a silent sigh as she slowly twisted the

deadbolt on the door. The 'click' seemed to reverberate like a gunshot but only in her mind. She paused for a full minute and pointed her hearing towards her roommates room. Nothing, so she eased the door open as Idris walked briskly down the hall.

He placed a quick kiss on her lips and headed straight for her bedroom as she attempted to close the door as quietly as it opened. She didn't bother with the lock since there was a man in the house. Plus security was tight and no one was getting in without approval.

Kelondra giggled when she reached her room to find Idris was already naked. This was a booty call after all so he only wore sweatpants, a wife beater and slides. She was prepped for a booty call as well and only wore a T-shirt and panties, minus the panties. She pulled the shirt over her head and was just as naked as he was.

Idris pulled her on the bed and dove face first between her legs. He got a lot of pussy but this was by far the best, cleanest and tastiest of them all. That's why he left a chick sleeping in his bed to come smash real quick.

"Sss," Kelondra hissed when his tongue got to twirling. He licked, lapped and sucked until she reached a squirming, squealing orgasm. She had to clamp her hand over her own mouth to muffle her whimpers.

"Been looking forward to this all day..." Idris said as he worked himself inside of her tightness. The slow entry was false advertising though because as soon as he snuggled inside he went to work. Kelondra bit down on her pillow to stifle her moans but the skin slapping echoed through the quiet apartment.

'Pap, pap, pap...' in the distance woke Vonda from her

sleep. She was having pleasant dreams of scams gone good until curiosity lifted her head from the pillow. Her TV wasn't on so she turned her head to the door. The soft sounds of sex carried on the air conditioned air as she stepped out of her room.

Now it was her turn to creep across the living room while listening out. The 'paps' grew louder and quicker the closer she got. She leaned her ear against the door and heard the unmistakably sounds of sex from within.

"I'm about to bust!" Idris warned. He was really asking permission to bust inside of her. Kelondra nodded just in the nick of time because he exploded a millisecond later. "Fuck!"

"You just did," she snickered and kissed his face as he writhed inside of her. Vonda just twisted her lips and crept back across the room.

Idris let out a double edged sigh at the inevitable. He hated to have to pull out of that good, wet, snug box but had too. He was ready to go straight to sleep after busting a nut, but now had to drive home. Kelondra provided a warm wash cloth so he could clean the good loving off his dick before putting it away.

"Wait," she whispered as she crept out of her room and across the livingroom. Once she eased the door open she waved him on. He rushed out and popped another kiss on her lips on the way out.

Kelondra retreated to the bathroom to soak her sore vagina for next time.

THERE WASN'T much talk as the roommates rode the next morning. Kelondra was reminiscing about the good sex she just had while Vonda wasn't sure how she felt about it. Complaining would seem like jealousy but she wasn't just jealous. She felt more betrayed than anything since she thought they were closer than they obviously were. Her shoulders shrugged on their own when she decided not to care. They were getting money and that was more important. The GPS announced their destination and she led the way.

"What is this place?" Kelondra asked as Vonda used the key to let them enter an apartment in an apartment complex. Her nose was still in the air even though the complex was decent.

"Don't worry, we not finna live here!" Vonda huffed in her native hood tone. It always came out when she was offended. She would certainly live here after coming from where she came from but her friend had her nose in the air.

"Oooooh!" Kelondra suddenly remembered. Now it was more than sufficient to do what needed to be done. They would use this address as the residence of their victims so they could get deliveries. It was rented with the information from one of their victims so it would only last a couple of months. More than enough time to make a killing and move on.

"We still need someone to sit here and collect packages. These damn package thieves don't play!" Vonda complained in a classic 'pot calling the kettle black' moment. She didn't want anyone stealing what they stole.

"How about, your sisters? They seem..." Kelondra offered then tapered off at the look on her face. "Or not..."

"Not! Definitely not," Vonda laughed. They would be

perfect since they rarely went to school. They just couldn't be trusted and weren't the brightest. There really wasn't much that could go wrong but Panda and Miranda would find a way to fuck it up. Another person came to mind who could certainly handle it but the thought scrunched her face and shook her head. Sheronda would be perfect but Sheronda was too greedy. Well enough is never enough for a greedy person.

"We'll figure it out," Kelondra was sure. She loved being a bad girl and taking chances. The sneaking around with Idris made her come that much harder.

It would have to wait since they had another party to attend. All those new clothes needed somewhere to be seen.

CHAPTER ELEVEN

Vonda vacillated as she dressed for the night on the town. She was proud to be a virgin but horny at the same time. Her box bubbled when she heard the sounds of sex coming through her roommate's door but wasn't sure what to do about it. She sure wouldn't mind having Steven eat her out again but he was stuck in a federal jail awaiting trial on federal child porn charges.

"Hmp!" she huffed defiantly when she decided to find someone else who would eat her out. That would be as far as she would allow since she still wasn't ready to have sex. She wasn't necessarily saving it for marriage, just wasn't giving it up tonight either. All the men she watched come and go inside her mother made her want more out of her love life.

"What's wrong?" Kelondra asked when Vonda came out with a look of determination etched on her face. They were just going to another frat party but she looked like it was the championship.

"Who?" Vonda asked and shook the look off her face. She cracked her best smile as proof that she was fine. "I'm fine!"

"You sure are!" Kelondra gushed as she complimented
her. In her defense she wanted to be a good friend but was
too spoiled. Some people make fucked up friends simply
because they don't know any better.

"So are you," Vonda smiled and sighed. She wanted to be
mad but girls like compliments. Her spirits lifted as high as
her esteem and they set out to go party. "I need to get a car!"

"You can now that we have the place," she shot back.
Turbo was building a few credit profiles that would be worth
hundreds of thousands of dollars. He was setting up
accounts and business fronts to handle the big money at their
fingertips.

"Dang," Vonda declared. Life was good and getting
better. She was out the hood and making plenty of money.
She was acing her classes and all was right with the world.
Now, if she could just find someone to eat her out.

Melvin came to pick them up and drop them off. He was
on call for when they were ready to leave so he could take
them home. This party was at one of the black frat houses
which dashed Vonda's hopes of getting her coochie licked
since brothers swear they don't kiss or eat pussy. At least in
days gone by because this new generation eats ass and sucks
dicks.

The roommates were dressed to impress so they braced
themselves to be smothered as soon as they entered the frat
house. Kelondra couldn't wait to scrunch her face like Vonda
did and say 'un-uh' like Vonda does. Some days she could out
Vonda even Vonda but only because Vonda was busy being
Kelondra. Except no rush of men was coming.

"What the what?" Kelondra wondered at the lack of
attention but Vonda quickly figured it out.

"Becky 'ndem," she said and nodded towards the pack of white girls getting all the attention. They all heard of the magical white girl's head and wanted in.

"Tuh!" her friend huffed and went straight for the punch bowl. Vonda could only shake her head as she filled her cup. Her focus shifted when she felt a tap on her shoulder. She spun to read the tapper his rights since no one likes to be tapped on the shoulder. "Um, is there a tap sign on my shoulder?"

"My bad. I just wanted some attention," the man apologized and raised his hands in surrender.

"I'm surprised you not chasing Suzy and Katie and Mandy..." she teased while looking him over. He was the opposite spectrum of pretty from Idris with his nearly yellow skin tone. The hazel eyes matched the sandy hair and he was pretty nonetheless.

"I'm not really into white girls," he said and shrugged like it was true. His mother was white but unlike his daddy he preferred some melanin. What was true was his ass was competing for their deep throats and long tongues too but lost out to football players.

"Mmhmm. I heard about that white girl head y'all love so much," she said and twisted her lips as a dare for him to deny it. He just smiled since she was right. "I feel you cuz them white boys tongue be, Mph!"

"Oh, so you fuck white boys?" the man asked like he didn't fuck white chicks. He did and would fuck a blue chick if the ass was fat.

"Naw, but I let one eat me out before," she admitted and waited for an offer that didn't come.

"Oh, ok. Nice meeting you," he said, looking over her

shoulder. She turned to see what he was looking at and saw a group huddled around someone twerking on the dancefloor.

"Bet not be these damn girls!" Vonda growled and stomped over to make sure it wasn't her sisters. It wasn't, it was the only thing worse. "Mama!"

"Hold, on, baby. Let me, show, em, how to twerk, that, thang!" Sheronda grunted as she twerked that thang. The frat guys tossed bills at her as she shimmied and shook.

Never had Vonda been so happy to hear a song end. Once it did she pulled her mother away from the dancefloor to a chorus of boos and jeers for canceling the show abruptly.

"Chile what are you doing?" Sheronda demanded.

"Me? I'm at a college party cuz I'm going to college!" she answered and asked. "Now, what are you doing?"

"Same thang as your sisters. Hang out, get clothes, some credit cards..." she dared.

"Credit cards?" Vonda asked with such veracity her mother believed her. Plus she knew her twins had sticky fingers. "Look, I do have a lick but..."

"But what?" Sheronda needed to know so she would know what lie to tell to overcome it.

"But I got other people down. You can get down but," she paused to figure the best way to word it. "But you don't run shit! You do what I say, and take what I give you!"

"Ok!" Sheronda backed down in surrender. "What I gotta do?"

VONDA WAS busy filling her mother in on the lick. Her end was simple but necessary. She would post up in the apartment and accept the deliveries. They would order plenty of personal items but Turbo had a connect that paid seventy five percent of retail for the computer hardware and software he bought. Enough to fill all of their pockets.

Sheronda listened intently while listening for a way to scheme and scam more out of the kids. She would play ball and play her position only long enough to get into position to run shit. Meanwhile, Kelondra was getting pissy drunk in a frat house. That can only end up one way.

"Whoa lil mama!" a football player exclaimed when a drunken Kelondra stumbled into him.

"Mmmah!" she giggled as she popped a kiss on his lips. Next thing she knew her feet left the ground when he picked her up over his shoulder.

"Looks like Bama got him one!" one of his teammates laughed as he carried the giggling girl away.

"Shit, got us one you mean," the other teammate corrected and followed them up to a room. He was followed by even more teammates, ready to put in some team work.

"Get the camera out!" someone said since the difference between a gang rape and a gang bang all goes down to the video tape.

Kelondra wasn't sober enough to give consent so the videos could work for or against the team. She was in and out of consciousness when the first man fucked her. She had no idea about the other six until later.

"WHAT'S WRONG WITH YOU?" Vonda asked and matched the sour puss on her friend's face.

What was wrong was beyond words so Kelondra just extended the thing that had her stuck for the last half an hour. Vonda reached for it until she realized what is was. There was no need to touch it since she could see the results from there. "Nuh-uh!"

"Yes-huh," Kelondra sighed and looked back down at the positive pregnancy test. She shook it again and looked again but it still said she was pregnant.

"Idris?" Vonda asked even though she was quite sure. Neither went on dates but she had been sneaking around with him for months. Thinking they got away with sneaking him in and out led to her sneaking him in and out even more.

"You know?" Kelondra reeled. She seemed more shocked about her secret affair than the plus sign in her hand. And as much as she encouraged Idris to come in her she bet not be surprised to be pregnant.

"Been knew," she shrugged and monitored how she felt about it. There was still no jealousy but still felt some kind of way about the behind her back act. Then, turn to her when she was in trouble. Even still, she would still help her friend. "So, what now?"

"Now I need to set up an appointment. I'm not having no dang baby!" Kelondra declared. Vonda nodded and agreed to help. She was a friend and that's what friends were for.

"What does he have to say about it?" Vonda asked.

"Hmp!" she huffed since Idris wouldn't take her calls or reply to her messages. She left voicemail, text, inbox and DMs but got no reply. She even emailed but that went unanswered as well.

"You need to tell him. It's only right," Vonda sighed. She was mad at her friend for allowing this and mad at herself for caring. It was her friend's sneaking around behind her back that got her into it, but here she was trying to help her get out of this.

"He is not talking to me. Ion even know why?" Kelondra moaned. She remembered waking up with a battered vagina after the party but assumed he was the reason why.

"Well, he'll talk to me!" Vonda fussed and stood. She began her march towards the front door until she saw Kelondra hadn't budged. "Come on chile!"

"Oh! Yeah..." she said and fell in step behind her. Kelondra wondered for a second how Vonda knew exactly how to get to Idris's apartment. Her mind actually had the audacious assumption that she and he were creeping behind her back. It took another second to recall Vonda met him first. "Oh yeah!"

"You are so strange!" Vonda laughed at the outburst. It would be the only words spoken until they parked at his building.

Both were relieved to see someone entering ahead of them so they wouldn't have to announce their presence. If Idris wouldn't take her calls he certainly wouldn't buzz them in. They looked like they belonged so the tenant ahead actually held the door for them.

"Thank you," Vonda extended. She got a kick out of being mannerable. Words like, thank you, excuse me, and please were far and few in between in the household she came from. The elevator ride only took seconds and they were ringing his doorbell.

"Excuse me," Idris told his latest friend as he excused himself to answer the door. He expected his DoorDash but got a surprise when he pulled it open. "The fuck?"

"This the fuck!" Vonda shot back and thrust the positive pregnancy test in his face.

"That's definitely not mine!" he laughed since he knew he hadn't touched her. Vonda turned to her friend and saw Kelondra hadn't barged in behind her. She reached back into the hallway and pulled her in.

"Tell him!" she demanded. Kelondra opened her mouth to speak but Vonda wasn't finished. "Mmhm. Sneaking around and screwing my roommate just cuz I ain't put out! Now look!"

"Look at what?" his lady friend asked as she came from the rear.

"He got my friend pregnant! Now won't take her calls! He ain't even answer her email!" Vonda fussed while Kelondra listened and nodded. "Same way he finna do you! Screw you, then it's, screw you!"

"Well?" his friend asked and tilted her head.

"Well nothing! That could be anybody's damn baby! How in the world could you know who's it is?" he asked with venom dripping down his chin. Kelondra reeled like she had been slapped. Because harsh words can sting like a backhand pimp slap.

"I, you, we..." Kelondra stammered before she could muster up the words. "You are the only one I've been with!"

"Hold that thought..." he said and pulled out his phone. It wasn't enough to find what he was looking for, he turned the hundred inch TV on and synced it to the phone.

All heads turned to the TV as the video began to play. The room went silent save the laughter from the men in the room, the squeaking of the bed and slapping of skin. It proved nothing until it zoomed in and showed Kelondra's face. Her head was rolled to the other side so it didn't show her eyes were closed at the moment.

"Oh Ki-ki!" Vonda moaned like a wounded animal. Her heart broke to see her friend being gang banged on the screen. She remembered finding her sleeping on the sofa where the players had left her. She was so used to carrying the drunk girl home she thought nothing of it. Proof you can save someone from everyone except themselves.

'Next!' a man laughed as the one inside of Kelondra finished up. He rolled off and she was quickly filled up again.

"And you want to put a baby on me!" Idris laughed and stung her again.

"They..." Vonda began when she noticed the men all wore condoms. She quickly realized that didn't make much of a defense. Kelondra was stuck in place from the shock until Vonda guided her away. "Come on."

"Yeah, go on, get!" he laughed as they headed for the door. His new friend followed right behind them. "Hey! Where are you going?"

"Home. Cuz, Mm-mm," she said, shaking her head. He made his point but still turned her off. His shoulders shrugged since this was Atlanta after all. A sea with plenty of fish.

CHAPTER TWELVE

"That's the sister right there..." Latisha Adams announced as Vonda stepped from the building.

"Yeah," Johnson grunted and didn't bother to look up.

Neither of them were particularly interested in the case at first. Two young girls with hot credit cards weren't much of a case and left no room to make any money for themselves. The card was linked to the growing number of fraud cases stemming from the Atlanta Tech student body. Finding out the twins had a sister who attended the school was a lead they had to follow up on.

"Looks like one of our suspects," she said as she compared the surveillance pictures of the girls using the hot cards. A moment later another familiar face stepped out of the building as well.

"Think that's the..." Johnson was saying until he registered the face.

"Is that the preppy victim's sister?" Latisha asked and snapped her fingers to help bring the name to mind.

"Worthington. Kenneth Worthington and that's the sister

Kelondra," he added. His partner snapped her head in his direction since he was never good with names. "I know the mother."

"I should have guessed," she said and shook her head. She remembered the mother was quite a looker so she wasn't surprised. What did surprise her was that she was definitely the second girl in the footage. The wigs and glasses may have fooled the clerks but the trained detectives saw right through them. "Well that doesn't make much sense?"

"Probably just for kicks," he surmised. "Background on the Perry girl showed she comes from a family of hustlers. Her mother has been arrested for fraud, shoplifting, bad checks..."

"She's the weak link then," Latisha nodded. They knew they wouldn't get anywhere with Vonda but the rich girl would fold under the slightest pressure.

"Let's follow and see where they lead..." he said and pulled out behind them.

"I NEED A DRINK," Kelondra sighed as she rode in the passenger seat of her own car.

"That's the last thing you need!" Vonda reeled and swerved. She thought about pulling over and just giving her a good old fashioned ass whooping. Sometimes, some people just need their asses whooped to help learn a lesson.

"Guess I need to wait until after the..." she sighed.

"Abortion! Until after the abortion!" Vonda snapped at the word she wouldn't say. It was her constant state of denial that got her into situations like this. What Vonda didn't know was that people coming to her rescue only contributed to the problem. Kelondra didn't have to worry about falling since someone was always there to catch her.

Even now, Kelondra lifted her chin as if she were above all that was going on. Yes, she was about to abort the unwanted, accidental pregnancy but had no plans to change any of the behavior that got her here. Here as in the abortion clinic they just arrived at.

"You're not coming in?" she asked when Vonda pulled up to the entrance instead of parking.

"Next time," she quipped but it was missed by the girl. "Anyway, I'll be back."

"Alright," Kelondra sighed and stepped inside. She joined the throngs of women inside waiting to terminate pregnancies for a variety of reasons. Some were just reckless enough to let men fuck them raw, yet still be surprised when they miss a period. Others had other reasons so they took a number and waited their turn.

Vonda headed over to the apartment to collect the loot that had been delivered for the day. She closely monitored the various email accounts to track the various deliveries. Because she knew her mother well enough to know she would skim the scammers if she got a chance.

"Hey mama," she greeted as she came into the apartment. It was completely loaded with loot from a variety of stores.

"Hey," Sheronda replied from one of the two leather sectional sofas in the living room. There were three dining room sets in the dining room and four expensive mattresses in the bedroom. She watched her daughter's eyes go to the open box in front of her. "Why y'all keep getting all this, stuff?"

"Because..." Vonda was saying but cash said it best. She produced twelve grand from her purse and handed it over. "That's why."

"Oh, ok," Sheronda relented when the cash touched her palm. That, she understood very well. "I still needs me some thangs. Hook me up with one of them cards."

"You can buy whatever you want with your money," her daughter reminded. "Ain't no cards to get. This is the hustle. Free money!"

"I know you better watch how you talk to me tho," Sheronda hissed. One might think she would be grateful for the free money after all the foul things she's had to do for money. One would be wrong too because the woman still wanted more.

"You right. My bad, I'll ask if we can get you one," Vonda relented. She was lying but it beat arguing or fighting. What she wasn't going to do was give the reckless woman a card.

"SHE'S COMING OUT," Latisha warned as Vonda came back out of the apartment she and Johnson followed her to.

"She sure doesn't look like a Nguyen Yi to me," Johnson remarked since that was the name the unit was listed to.

"Loaded down too." his partner added as she moved the deliveries to the trunk of the car. When it filled she used the back seat. They now had a dilemma as to whether they should follow Vonda or keep an eye on the apartment.

"Look," Latisha pointed at the UPS truck that hissed to a stop right in front of the building. Adam pulled up the binoculars and watched as the driver approached the door.

"Sho nuff!" he laughed when he saw Sheronda open the door and sign for the package.

"A family affair," she said, shaking her head. Sure enough Vonda collected that package too and put it in the car. The question was answered so they gave Vonda a few second headstart and pulled out after her.

Vonda was too green to notice she was being tailed. Blasting the music didn't help matters either. She happily led the police straight to Turbo to transfer the loot. He would fence it through his network and split the cash. She also collected a few more cards for her and Kelondra to burn through but nothing for her mother.

"Tag, you're it," Latisha said of Turbo as he became the subject of the tail. They rode in silence back out to West View where Turbo pulled into the driveway of a three quarter million dollar home.

"Zack Steinberg," Johnson said as he ran the address and identified the occupants. "He may be our guy?"

"Perhaps. We just have to shed some dead weight," Latisha agreed. Once Vonda and Kelondra were out of the way they could work the nerd for themselves. "Ready for warrants?"

"Not quite yet. Just one more thing I need to nail down," Johnson said.

"What, warn the mother like the Rollins kid?" she shot back. She eventually got over him, warning Sinclair since they were still getting money together. That didn't stop her from bringing it up, every chance she got.

"Huh? Nah, you can have the Worthington girl. The father will buy her way out of trouble," he replied. His mind was on the other mother.

❄

"COMING..." Sheronda called out to the chime of the doorbell. She waved a can of air freshener around the smokey room but it did little to dissipate the weed smoke. Sheronda was foolish enough to smoke up an apartment used to receive stolen merchandise. She opened the door for the driver but found a detective standing there instead.

"Well, well, well..." Johnson laughed as he walked in on top of her. He didn't know the woman started to make a break for it but blocked the door with his body.

"I was just visiting and I'm finna go!" she insisted and tried to squeeze around him.

"Except you've been under surveillance for weeks. Signed for tens of thousands of dollars worth of stolen merchandise. Shall I go on?" he asked and closed the door behind him.

"I guess you want some pussy," she sighed since she knew cops and cops like pussy. Plus this one flirted pretty heavily when they met. Add that to the fact that he was here alone and, "Yeah, you want some."

"Why not," he laughed and followed her over to one of the sofas in the crowded room. He dropped his pants and sat his ass on the leather while she stripped out of her jeans. She shook her head and the flaccid dick and knew he was getting some head and tail.

Johnson leaned back and enjoyed the show as she inhaled the dick. He tore the condom wrapper open with his mouth as he started to grow stiff in her mouth. Soon she had a full fledged erection in her mouth so she spit it out.

Sheronda watched as he rolled the rubber on and checked the tip.

"Hope you know how to ride..." he said as she mounted the dick like a cowgirl mounting her horse.

"Hmp!" Sheronda huffed at the dare. If some pussy was going to keep some handcuffs off her wrist he was about to get the ride of his life. She planned to show out so she stood on his thighs and lowered herself on his dick until he reached the bottom. "Yee-haw!"

Johnson could only hold her small waist as she whipped her hips. Back and forth, side to side and up and down. Sheronda really showed out when she did a spin and began to ride him backwards. All he could do was hold on for the ride. She even surprised herself when she bust a good nut of her own. The shiver sent Johnson over the edge as well.

"Shit!" he fussed as he went stiff and filled up the condom. "Damn it man!"

"Can I ride? Tuh!" Sheronda laughed and stood up off the dick. His wet dick and full condom was his problem not hers so she went into the bathroom to clean herself up.

Johnson was used to fucking on the fly so he pulled out his kit to clean up. The rubber went into a zip lock bag and a wet wipe wiped the residue from his pubic hair and balls. He was stepping back outside by the time Sheronda finished washing up for her date with Slim.

"All units, suspect is present. Move in," he said into his police radio. On cue, cars pulled from several directions to make the arrest.

"You're ridiculous," Latisha laughed and shook her head. A few minutes later Sheronda was brought out in cuffs and taken away.

"Her reverse doggy style was ridiculous!" he laughed as they went in to process the scene. It was the first of many arrests to come. Sheronda used her one call to call the twins to let them know to watch Shay and David until she returned. Their first call went to Vonda.

CHAPTER THIRTEEN

"Shit!" Vonda sighed when Melvin pulled into the stash apartment parking lot. Police were still loading stolen merchandise into a police truck. She made a beeline here after getting off the phone with the twins. She just knew something her mother did caused the whole cookie to crumble.

"What's wrong?" he asked over to the passenger seat.

"Nothing. Take me to the dorm," she demanded, then changed her mind. "No, the house."

By now the driver knew 'the house' meant her mother's house so he headed to the hood. He was all ears but Vonda wasn't talking. Her mind scrambled to figure out what was going on and why. Had Sheronda done something crazy or was the whole operation compromised? She pulled her phone and called Kelondra to see what she knew but hung up after one ring.

"Your friend just rang," Latisha told Kelondra since her hands were cuffed behind her back. Police had pulled her over for a traffic violation at the detectives directive. What they didn't want was a big scene at the dorm that could alert any other people involved. "She hung up. Guess you'll have to take all the charges by yourself?"

"No wait! I'll tell you whatever you need to know," she vowed. "It was my roommate's idea! She made me do it!"

Handcuffs have that effect on some people. Kelondra was some people and began to spill her guts on the whole operation right there on the side of the street where they pulled her over. The two detectives looked at each other when she got to Turbo. They gave a tacit nod at what had to be done. It was good she snitched off the record so they could keep Turbo for themselves.

"Need me to stay?" Melvin asked when he saw two stone faced men in the front yard.

"Nah, that's just Slim and Rayford. My mama's nigga-in-laws," she sighed and paid him for the ride. She hopped out and headed over to see what the men knew.

"The police not saying nothing!" Rayford moaned. He had a pocket full of stripper money to bail Sheronda out but she hadn't been processed. There was no record of an arrest as of yet.

"This is crazy!" Slim protested. It was his day and this was cutting into it. "Let's just go down there!"

"Ride with me!" Rayford agreed. The nigga-in-laws mounted up and rode out to save their woman. Meanwhile Vonda marched into the house to get to the bottom of it.

"What the fuck happened!" Vonda barked as she stormed into the house she no longer lived in.

"No idea," Kirby said and snapped his head towards the twins since he knew they did.

"Mama got locked up for some credit card," Panda shrugged and was done talking.

"Not the one we got from y'all 'partment tho!" Miranda added to be helpful. She winked and nodded to her twin like she did good.

"I know y'all heifers ain't fuck up my whole lick over a burned out card!" Vonda reeled in disbelief. The more she thought about it the worse it got. "After, after I bought y'all bitches some clothes!"

"You the bitch, bitch!" Panda snapped. Constantly getting called a bitch by their mother was more than enough. They were forced to take it from Sheronda, but anyone else was in for a fight.

"Bitch!" Vonda reiterated and attacked. She took off on her sister with both fist flying but Panda fought back. Plus, there were two of them. Miranda loved her big sister but shared a brain with her twin. It was pure instinct that propelled her hands and jumped her own sister. The once fair fight became lopsided in a second. Luckily Kirby was close by to break it up.

"Y'all get off of her!" he shouted and shoved one twin. Then snatched Vonda away from the other. "Y'all are sisters!"

"Fuck them bitches! I put you on and you steal from me!" Vonda shouted as he corralled the twins to keep them off of her.

"Bitch you just for yourself!" Panda shouted while Miranda added. "You left us!"

"And I'm finna leave y'all again!" the elder sister shouted. She suddenly became calm and lifted her chin. "On God I ain't never finna step foot in this house again."

"Good! Don't come back!" Panda shouted after her as she

walked out of the house. Miranda didn't join in this time since that was the last thing she wanted. Her heart broke a little bit knowing her sister was telling the truth. If she ever saw her again it would be coincidence or accident. She was never coming back.

"HEY THERE, VONDA?" Latisha asked casually as she approached Vonda when she got out of Melvin's car. She wanted to be discreet and not cause a scene at the dorm, if she could help. If Vonda would allow it that is.

"Who? Naw, Ion know her," she said and turned to make a break. Johnson was standing in that direction and cut off her escape.

"Let's do this the easy way," he warned.

"Your mom and friend are waiting down at the station. Come take a ride. You'll be back before dinner," Latisha offered.

"Am I under arrest?" Vonda dared.

"You will be if, I have to chase you," Latisha assured her. Vonda looked around at her fellow students milling about. She didn't want to be the talk of the dorm so she let out a sigh and complied. Besides, if they wanted to arrest her they would have. As many times as Sheronda's door had been kicked down while growing up she knew better.

"Maaaaaan!" she moaned and got into the car. The ride over to the precinct was made in silence. The cops couldn't talk in front of the suspect and the suspect didn't have shit to say to the cops.

Cops are master manipulators and had everything set up

when they arrived. Kelondra was seated in a room eating Chick Fila while Sheronda was in another sipping a soda. Both seemed more comfortable and relaxed than they should be for people in trouble.

"Soda?" Johnson asked with a sliver of sarcasm since her mother was drinking one.

"Chicken sandwich?" Latisha added with mirth on her mouth. "I hear they're pretty good."

"I'ma get my own chicken and soda once I get out of here," Vonda snipped. She was ready to get to it so she could get out of there.

"Yeah, they might be eating instant chicken pills, like the Jetsons by the time you get out!" Johnson laughed but the two females were too young to catch the joke. He shrugged his shoulders and turned his laptop to face her. "Anyway..."

'It was all my roommate's idea! I just did what she told me...' Kelondra confessed. Vonda just blinked in disbelief as she gave up every minute detail. She remixed her involvement and threw Sheronda under the same bus as her roommate. The recording abruptly stopped when they reached Turbo.

"Oh, and this..." the detective said and pulled up the next interview. Vonda lifted her head in pride when she saw her mama on the screen. The same mama who taught them not to snitch on anything, ever.

"This whole thang was my daughter's idea. The girl been trouble since..." Sheronda moaned like a victim. It took a few takes to get it right but the performance was perfect.

"Wow," Vonda said and shook her head. Her future just crumbled right before her eyes but she lifted her head anyway. She would take her lick like a boss and move on.

"Who is Turbo?" Latisha asked offhandedly. Johnson pretended to scribble notes on his notepad but was actually drawing pictures of pussies. Both listened intently for her answer because a lot was riding on it.

"I think it's something to do with the engine?" Vonda asked in her ditzy Kelondra imitation. The transfer of personalities went both ways and she could do Kelondra better than Kelondra could.

"Who is this then!" Johnson demanded and slammed the picture of the hacker on the table.

"Um, Justin Beber?" she wondered and twisted her curls. The detectives had heard enough and smiled.

"Good answer," Latisha nodded. "Now you see how quickly your people threw you under the bus?"

"Your own mama!" Johnson instigated unnecessarily since Vonda was done with Sheronda and the twins. Kirby was old enough to stay in touch but Shay and David would have to do without her.

"Now, you and Turbo, you're going to work with us..." Latisha explained. Vonda twisted her lips and cocked her head at first. She slowly untwisted and uncocked as she laid out their plan. A plan that could net millions with police resources and protection. By the end of her spiel the girl was in.

"CAN I GO NOW?" Sheronda asked when Johnson entered the room.

"Yup," he said and stood aside.

"Should press charges on your ass for stealing some

pussy!" she fussed at being tricked out some pussy before the raid. He was supposed to go in and survey the scene but fucked her instead.

"That would be crazy since the pussy is why you can go," he lied. "We're not pressing charges."

"Shit is good huh?" Sheronda asked. She didn't get many compliments beyond having some good pussy or fiyah head so she relished in them.

"The best," he said over his shoulder as he headed down the hall. Sheronda stepped out to find her worried nigga-in-laws waiting anxiously.

"You good?" Slim wanted to know while Rayford rushed forward to hug her. Sheronda opened her mouth to speak but got stuck when she saw her daughter. They glared at each other for a moment, until Vonda broke it off. She conceded the staring battle since she was winning the war. She lifted her head and spun on her heels to call Melvin to pick her up. Meanwhile, Madelyn Worthington had just arrived to collect her daughter.

"What, what's going on?" the woman demanded. She received a call from her daughter in jail and rushed downtown to save the day. Kelondra opened her mouth to confess but Johnson beat her to it.

"Seems like a big misunderstanding. She's been very helpful!" he said and nodded with Kelondra to make sure she caught on.

"Uh, yeah. Misunderstanding, big," she repeated and squinted to make sure she was seeing clearly.

"You know I would never let anything happen to her on my watch!" Johnson declared and puffed out his chest.

"I know. Thank you!" Madelyn gushed and reached for her daughter's hand.

"You can thank me later," he winked. She nodded and led her only child out of the precinct.

"You're moving home!" Madelyn declared as she drug her child from the station.

"No, I..." Kelondra protested until her mother snatched her off the ground and pinned her to the wall. The police looked, then quickly looked away. More kids need to be snatched off their feet by their parents. Sure beats prisons and graveyards.

"No, my ass!" she growled as if she might bite. "We're going to the dorm to collect your things and we're going home!"

"Yes mother," Kelondra relented. She had nearly been gang raped, been pregnant and just dodged prison. And it was only freshman year. She began to nod as they exited the police station. "Yeah, I want to go home."

VONDA WAS RELIEVED to see the empty parking spot when she arrived back at the dorm. Melvin had been yacking the whole way over and it's good there wouldn't be a test on it because she didn't hear a word of it.

Hearing her so-called friend selling her out had her drunk. Hearing her mother do the same was sobering. Combined she was in a state of what the fuck. Adding the cops proposal's to get money with them made the day even stranger.

Turbo came running when she called him, only to be

ambushed by the crooked detectives. He too jumped at the chance to do what he does best with impunity. It was a license to steal and the cops had the databases to provide an endless flow of names and numbers for him to work.

They liked the way Vonda worked it and how cool she stayed under pressure. Not only didn't she blink when her mother sold her out. She stuck her chest out, ready to take her lick without snitching on anyone else.

Now she had to face the friend who just sold her out. She wasn't sure how she was supposed to live with it and her but had nowhere else to go. After just cutting her sisters off she had no problems cutting anyone else off.

"Finna get my own 'partment!" she muttered as she entered the building. The blast of ice cold air knocked some sense into her head since units like this would cost a couple thousand dollars a month. "Or not!"

Her thoughts were interrupted when she reached her unit and saw the door was opened. Her mind flashed to Kelondra's empty parking spot. That equaled an intruder and she had taken enough losses for the day. She rushed in, fist balled, on the fuck shit.

"Ion know who the fuck..." she growled, ready to bite. She stopped dead in her tracks when she came face to face with Mr Worthington. He tilted his head curiously, but still glanced at her breast as his ex wife came out.

"We're just here for Kelondra's belongings! We don't want any problems!" Mrs Worthington insisted. She took her ex husband's hand as she came to his side.

"Your daughter has all the problems you need. Trust and believe!" she said and hurried into her own bedroom.

The Worthington parents had come together to save

their last remaining child. The streets would eat her just like it had their son. The hand holding was because he realized he was needed at home. They reconciled for the sake of their daughter.

They loaded Kelondra's clothes and personal items into the car and headed back out to the burbs. Vonda would be riding solo for the rest of the school year. A win/win since both girls were bad influences on the other.

"Is that, the cop?" Mr Worthington wondered when they stepped outside to see detective Johnson parked out front.

"Yes?" she asked since she wasn't sure how he kept popping up wherever she was. He looked at her ex husband and pulled away. "There's something I need to tell you..."

Madelyn filled him in on the way home where Kelondra was waiting. However, she wasn't the only one going home.

CHAPTER FOURTEEN

"So, what's the first thing you finna do when you hit the city?" Chino asked and braced himself for some exotic answer. The man had been gone ten years before Marquis even came to prison so he just knew he was going to do it big.

"Prolly finna fuck some big booty hoes!" Larry cheered. He really liked big booty hoes, but then again, who doesn't.

"Get some chicken!" a large man called Big Chicken proclaimed. He earned his moniker because he was big and liked chicken. He was such a fan of chicken that the paltry leg quarter served once a month just didn't cut it. So he went around the chow hall knocking people out and taking their chicken as well. Twenty years later people just give him their leg quarter to avoid the nap. Chicken is good but no one wants to get knocked out for it.

"All that!" Marquis laughed and nodded. He would do those things for his friends who would never get a chance to do them again.

Chino caught a life sentence for killing a man who robbed and tried to kill him. He would have gotten an award and medal for it in most states but Georgia gave him a life sentence. Larry actually earned his multiple life sentences for the multiple armed robberies he committed. Big Chicken killed his wife and the man he found in his wife, in his bed. He probably could have gotten a medal too, but not in Georgia.

Plus, Marquis liked chicken and big booty hoes as much as the next man. He had a slew of chicks who held him down during his bid so he owed them some dick. Especially the ones who filled the void after Marquita quit and filled their vaginas with drugs to smuggle into the prison.

"You ready?" the officer asked when he came to collect Marquis. He replied by hopping to his feet and grabbing the bag of letters and cards. They were the only things he was taking with him. The rest of his belongings were evenly distributed amongst these three men.

"I'll holla later," Marquis said when he gave a last round of hugs. The bitter sweet part of leaving prison is leaving people you love behind. No one loves them enough to stay, so they leave.

Marquis processed out the prison and collected his debit card. The state of Georgia is generous enough to give departing inmates a whole thirty five dollars upon release. It didn't matter if they just served thirty five years, all they had coming was those thirty five dollars.

Georgia is one of the few states that don't pay inmates for labor. Most just leave with a full fledged drug addiction and thirty five dollars to fuel it. Quite a few would commit a crime on day one. Destined to forever revolve in this vicious cycle.

Not Marquis though since he was on the opposite side of

the meth pipes and blunts the inmates smoked to make life behind the wall bearable. An oxymoron if ever because life is unbearable behind the wall. The best one can do is find something to numb it down to a dull ache. Most use drugs, some find religion, others read, while this one writes.

Marquis sold drugs, tobacco and cell phones smuggled in through girl friends, officers and even a drone. He made more money than the warden and stacked it his whole bid. The twenty twenty two Benz that pulled up to collect him was his going home present to himself. The house he was paroling to was his too.

"In the back player!" Owen smiled when he approached the car. He had a present to present as well.

"Ok then!" Marquis laughed when he found the naked woman seated in the back. They hadn't gotten out of the parking lot before the tip of his dick touched her tonsils. "You got that info for me?"

"Yup. Shole do..." Owen nodded through the rear view. He was a loyal soldier who followed directions. Even the ones he didn't understand.

"GOOD MORNING AGAIN!" Carey cheered when he met his wife in the kitchen after a shower.

"Again!" she laughed since their first good morning came when he lifted her leg and slid inside of her when the alarm went off this morning.

"I may have to come home for lunch!" he said since he couldn't get enough of his new wife.

"I'll have it hot and ready for you," she promised. This

new wife was nothing like the old wife. The last Mrs Rollins was fucking everyone but him. This new one gave it to him whenever he wanted, and whenever she wanted. That was plenty.

Carey kissed the baby on his forehead and planted one on hers as well on his way out of the house. He blamed himself for the way his first son turned out and would not make the same mistakes this time. Fuck that job and anything that could interfere with taking care of them. A few minutes ticked off before a knock on the door disturbed mommy and baby time.

"Um, why are you knocking at your own house? When you have a key, and I am feeding your baby..." Marquita was saying as she answered the door. Her husband had just left a minute ago so she pulled the door open without bothering to see who was knocking. Her eyes went wide as she stumbled back into the house.

"Honey, I'm home!" Marquis laughed at her face. Marquita was too shocked for words and stumbled backwards. He took it as an invitation and entered behind her. He closed the door behind him and glared down at the child in her arms.

"What do you want?" she asked and pulled her baby to the side, away from his gaze.

"What's mine. I want everything that's mine," he said and took a seat. He leaned back and put his feet up on the coffee table.

"Ion know what that means?" Marquita snapped and pushed his feet off the table.

"The fuck you don't!" he exploded and flipped the table

before standing. "I left you with my son! Come back to no son and you got the next nigga son!"

"Marquis, you got the boy who did it! He's dead! What else you want!" she demanded.

"Like I said, everything that belongs to me..." he said and cupped her vagina.

"That doesn't belong to you!" she fumed and pushed his hand away. "Hasn't for a long time!"

"Yeah, cuz you let ole Leon get some," he recalled and laughed. "Until I had his shit splattered on the sidewalk!"

"You said you ain't kill him!" Marquita moaned. She was madder at herself for believing him over her own instinct. Marquis had threatened a few men away from her before Leon. He didn't scare off and she dated him.

"I told you, I'm here for everything that's mine," he repeated and sat again. The way he went from zero to a hundred, then back to zero scared her. As it should since only crazy folks can pull that off.

"I got a husband!" she pouted and pleaded.

"Same nigga who son killed our son!" he roared. She felt his pain since she felt it too. Felt the murderous rage that almost made her kill the wrong kid in the driveway.

"It's not his fault tho! The mother! It was the mother!" Marquita pleaded. She would gladly sell her out to save her husband. "She is the one who encouraged him! Carey ain't even like his son!"

"That's where I'll start. Where the mama stay?" Marquis inquired.

"Atlantic Station!" she shot back and quickly came off the info. She knew Sinclair's whereabouts by heart since her husband had to pay all her bills.

"Check..." Marquis said and looked her up and down. He looked over at the baby once more before walking out of the house.

Marquita ran for the phone to call her husband, then changed her mind. She decided to call the police but changed her mind again. The way he looked at her baby shook her to the core. She dead bolted the doors and took him up to her room. All she could do was wait.

"HEY BABE?" Carey asked instead of greeted when he came in from work. His new wife was usually at the door holding their baby when he came in. Marquita opted to work from home so she wouldn't have to choose between family or work. Not that it would be much of a choice since she loved her family. She loved her job too so she did it from the house.

"Huh?" Marquita asked since he was talking French, or German or something because she couldn't understand a word of it.

"Are you ok?" he asked and sat beside her. She was totally frazzled by the unexpected and unwelcome guess. What was even more confusing was Marquis still had another year or so left on his sentence. She checked periodically just to make sure and saw no mention of the early release. She knew this day would come, just not so soon.

"Who?" she asked and looked around curiously.

"Marquita, what's wrong? What happened?" Carey now insisted. After the craziness of the last year he wasn't sure what else could happen.

"Um, nothing," she decided and noticed the baby was

asleep in her arms. That gave her pause to take him over the the crib and lay him out. "Yeah, crazy day! This war and pandemic is killing my portfolios!"

"Tell me about it," Carey agreed and sighed. He quickly shook his own bad day off since he refused to bring work home again. He was man enough to recognize his own short-comings in his last relationship and man enough not to repeat them. Some days he would sit in the car in the driveway for a few minutes to decompress before coming inside.

"Don't worry about nuffin 'lil shawty," Marquita assured him in the hood persona he loved so much. She went for his zipper and whipped out the wood. "Big mama got you..."

"Mm-mm," Carey moaned and grew stiff inside his wife's mouth. He leaned back and loosened his tie since a blow job really isn't very formal. He gripped all that ass under her shorts as she bobbed her head. A finger slid under her panties and inside of her. It was so slick and slippery he needed to be inside of her. "Come here..."

"Mm-mm," she mimicked when he pulled her on top of him and slid her panties aside. She let him do the honors and insert himself inside. Once he did she sank slowly to the bottom of her box and began to rock.

The couple made eye contact as they made love on the living room sofa. Slow, passionate kisses accompanied the slow roll of her hips. Marquita soaked his lap when the plea-sure increased. It was a prelude to the orgasm creeping through her body.

"That's right..." Carey said knowingly. He gripped her ass and thrust upwards to meet her rolls. Her face contorted when she tried to fight it. Not that she didn't want it, it just came harder when she fought it.

"Fuck!" Marquita shouted and bust a nut. She fell over limply to the side but her husband was right with her. With her pleasure confirmed he could be selfish and focus on his own nut. He lifted her leg so he could watch the deep strokes he was delivering. That's how he saw her coat his dick in that good, creamy lotion good pussy manufactures. She came again and took him with her this time.

"Fuck!" Carey agreed since a good nut will make you say that. This one could very well be that second kid they were working on.

"I love you baby," Marquita moaned like she wanted to cry.

"I love you too baby. Is everything ok?" he had to ask again from her demeanor. This would have been an excellent time to come clean but she didn't.

"Mmhm, shole is," she offered in her southern belle voice to disarm him. Marquis was her problem and she would figure out how to deal with it. Besides, she fed him information on Sinclair and he wasn't going to do shit.

CHAPTER FIFTEEN

"Give me another!" Sinclair demanded and pounded her palm on the bar.

"We don't serve drunks!" the bartender shot back. She had tried to ignore the woman but her privileged attitude wouldn't allow it.

"How dare you! I..." the socialite huffed but the owner stepped in before she could puff and blow his bar down.

"One for the road in exchange for your car keys," he offered. This way he could shut her up as well eliminate any liability for his establishment.

"And just how, am I supposed to get home?" Sinclair challenged. She had to close one eye to stop seeing double and focus on the speaker. The man would do for what she needed next.

Life as a forty something divorcee in Atlanta wasn't quite what she expected. In fact, she got more action as a cheating wife than she had since the divorce.

Her ex and his new wife had a new baby in their new life. She had an expensive one bedroom apartment in the heart of the city and no life. Days were used to sleep off the late nights of heavy drinking. A vicious circle encircled her and threatened to swallow her alive.

She thought about hooking back up with detective Johnson and his Johnson but couldn't bring herself to make the call. He tried to help but was still a reminder of the son she just lost to prison violence. Any thoughts of Carey junior drove her to drink, and the last thing a drunk needs is another reason to drink.

"Uber?" he offered but she didn't bite. He did notice her noticing him and gave her a once over as well. The alcohol use only made her look her age but didn't detract from her banging body. She could get it, so he offered it. "Where do you live? Maybe I can drop you?"

"You sir, have a deal!" she cheered in a slur and handed over her car keys. He gave the nod to the bartender and only got an eye roll in reply. If the owner wanted his own rules broken he would have to break them himself. He grabbed a glass and did just that.

"Apple martini," he stated, more than asked since he knew what she usually drank. She nodded happily as he shook and poured her poison.

"Thank you!" she sang and tossed it back. Sinclair hopped down from her perch on the barstool and was ready to go. "Ready!"

"Would you mind locking up Sheila?" he asked and got another eye roll. He took that one as a yes and slid the keys down the bar.

"This way..." Sinclair slurred and pointed left. The man twisted his lips at the adjacent high rise in walking distance and realized he had been tricked out of some dick. Getting some pussy was a consultation prize so he shrugged it off and walked with her.

Come to find out she really did need an escort since the city was becoming more dangerous by the day. Plus she was pissy drunk and he had to keep her from veering into the street. He helped her into her building and up to her floor.

"These are nice!" the bar owner nodded in approval.

"Thanks to my ex!" she cheered since the generous divorce settlement allowed her to live comfortably on his dime.

"Yeah, well..." he said and looked at his watch. He was ready to do what he came for so he could go home.

"Pushy, pushy for some pussy, pussy," Sinclair laughed and led him to her bedroom. She peeled off her clothes as she went and was naked when she reached the middle of her bed.

"Don't mind if I do!" he said when she tooted the booty up for back shots. Sinclair actually had a mean backshot arch but was waiting until he got inside of her to spring it on him.

He retrieved a condom with one hand and fondled the fat box with the other. Sinclair moaned and writhed as she soaked his fingers. He eagerly rolled the condom down the shaft of his dick and slid inside.

"Hard! Do it hard!" she demanded and hit him with the arch. He gripped her hips and complied. Filling the room with the wonderful sounds of skin slapping and pussy gushing. A few minutes later another sound filled the room.

"Huh?" he asked when her moans changed to another sound. He leaned around and looked forward to seeing she had fallen asleep in the act. Her soft snores soon filled the room. No real man wants it like that so he pulled out and cleaned himself up. His head shook at the round ass and plump, juicy vagina going to waste. His head was still shaking when he exited the building.

"Mmhm. Got yo ass..." Owen said as he took more pictures of the man he followed Sinclair home from the bar with. He would shoot them to his boss in the morning and his work was done. The target liked to take men home from the bar. That can be dangerous.

"GRRRR, GRRRR, GRRRR," Slim growled as he beat the box up. Sheronda's moans and squeaky bed drowned out the giggles of the twin girls peeking from the crack in the door.

"Get this pussy!" Sheronda demanded and pulled her legs even higher. Panda and Miranda both covered their mouths to stifle the snickers. Their eyes went wide with wonder when the couple changed positions.

"Dang!" they sang when Slim pulled nearly a foot of dick out of their mother. They blinked in disbelief at how much dick the skinny man was toting around in his skinny jeans. It was glistening in the light from the TV from mama's good juices.

Sheronda flipped over and tooted the booty up. Slim didn't even have to aim as he slid right back inside. He leaned back and delivered back shots that reverberated around the room. Knowing he had to share the pussy with his nigga-in-law always made him show out when it was his turn. Rayford had good money but his dick wasn't as long as this so Slim had an edge. Slim got his out the street so the ten grand in his pockets was his re-up to keep going.

The girls snickered again when he switched gears and really pounded the pussy. Sheronda collapsed under the pressure but Slim went with her and kept on humping. She squealed while he growled as the episode came to a mutually climatically end.

"Grrr, grrr, grrr," he repeated as he pumped her full of semen. It was payback since Rayford left her flooded on his last turn.

"A'ight now..." Sheronda warned and yawned. They wanted to compete by coming in her and she was going to hit them both up for some abortion money.

"Mmhm," Slim laughed and rolled over on his back. Their audience stifled another giggled when his dick flopped to the side. A moment later and both were snoring.

The twins didn't need a plan since it was custom. Fall asleep in this house and they were going through your pockets. Especially now that their mother had been crabbing more than usual. Now that Vonda cut her off she wasn't buying them anything. They had to get it like they lived so they eased into the room to the rhythm of their snores.

Both girls dropped low and literally slithered on the floor. Each took a pocket and went inside. They had to stop abruptly when Miranda made his keys jiggle on her side. Sheronda and Slim kept on snoring so they kept on digging.

Miranda came out with a ring but her sister shook her head. It was too big and had too many diamonds not to be a problem. Panda smiled at her bright idea and nodded at her mother's night stand. Miranda smiled when she caught on and placed the ring on top. This would deter the blame from them and they continued their search.

Panda's eyes went wide when her hand found a thick

wad. She prayed it was cash as she slowly withdrew it. The moment of truth came when it came out. They blinked at what was more money than they had seen in their young lives.

They had a tacit debate right there on the spot. It was a lot, but how much should they take? Both came to the same conclusion and nodded at their decision to take it all. They began to ease back out on their bellies but Miranda paused.

Her sister cocked her head curiously as she slowly lifted herself up. She leaned over to get a closer look at the dick. It was less intimidating when it was soft. The mutual juices had dried to a crust but she still had to touch it.

Panda shook her head and laughed, then touched it as well. Slim stirred from being molested and they hit the floor. The snores resumed so they slithered away the same way they came. They stayed low as they tiptoed to their room and closed the door.

"Dang!" they both sang when Panda produced the cash. Luckily for Miranda she didn't blink on the way or it would have been half of what it is.

"Count it!" Panda ordered since her counting and spelling wasn't the best.

"Dang!" Miranda said with each thousand dollars they reached. Ten dangs later they had a little over ten thousand dollars since Slim couldn't count that well either. He owed the connect ten racks but counted nearly eleven. Miranda saw no reason to come off the few hundred she found in the other pocket. Slim had it separate to give to their mother before he left. They split the remaining cash as even as they could since Panda couldn't add so a little more went to her sister.

"Let's go to granny's house. He gonna be mad when he wakes up," Miranda suggested. Her sister nodded in agreement since this was a lot of money. They always took money out of men's pockets but never this much. This would be a problem.

"Hell yeah," Panda agreed. They packed a spinna-night bag and headed out.

"Where y'all going?" Kirby wanted to know since he was as close to the man of the house as there would ever be.

"To mind our biz!" Panda fussed and scrunched her face up at him.

"To granny house. If mama asks we been there all night," Miranda said. She knew you can get more flies with sugar so she parted with a sweet twenty dollar bill.

"All night," he agreed and cuffed the cash. He took it to his stash and went back to bed.

CHAPTER SIXTEEN

"Mm-mm," Sheronda declined when Slim rubbed his morning wood on her back.

"Let a nigga get a nut 'fo the road," he said, raspy with desire. A good nut would be a nice start for a busy day of trapping. He had to go pay his connect so he could re-up. Then go home and cut crack, bag crack and sell crack. A good nut sure would help.

"What is this, some pitstop pussy!" she fussed. Weird because in actuality she was some pitstop pussy. A man can come through and smash in under a minute and move on. She even had a set of flags to direct traffic to her box if needed.

"Come on, let a nigga fuck real quick," he asked and spanked her bottom with his hard dick.

"Ok, first of all!" she giggled at the spanking.ain't no such thang as quick with that thang! And you know it's Rayford day. You gonna come in me anyway."

"Shit, he not finna check yo stomach , is he?" he asked since head was the next best thing.

"He might!" she laughed and rolled out the bed.

"Whatever," Slim fussed and rolled out too. He really should have showered the sex off but didn't. He found his drawers under the sheets and tucked the dick away. Sheronda used perfect timing when he picked up his pants to crack for some money.

"Let me hold a few dollars, for the light bill," she asked with her hand out since her niggas never said no.

"Should make you get it from Rayford. Since it's his damn day," Slim grumbled as he reached into the pocket where her money was. He went past his keys and found nothing. "The fuck?"

"What's wrong babe?" asked as he frantically dug into his other pocket.

"My bread..." he replied and checked the back pockets even though his mind replayed exactly where he put everything. Including the ring he bought for his mama. The same one Sheronda just picked up on the nightstand. "Bitch, you been in my pockets?"

"Bitch? Un-uh, that's what we not finna do!" she snapped but he was spazzing. Spazzing trumps snapping like rock does scissors.

"And you got my mama ring!" he screamed and ran across the bed. Sheronda had something to say about that but his hand around her throat made it wait. "Bitch that's my re-up money! I need my fucking money!"

"Ughargh!" she pleaded and tapped out. There was no ref to recognize the tap and stop the fight. Good thing he stopped on his own because he wanted answers. Rayford could have the bitch to himself now, he just needed his bread. It dawned on him that she couldn't tell him if she was dead so he loosed her esophagus. Sheronda gagged and coughed as she struggled to catch her breath.

"Where my bread hoe!" he demanded with a slap that helped her catch her breath. Now she didn't mind being called bitches and hoes. What was important was getting him his money back. And she knew just who took it.

"The twi, twins," she coughed and tried to call out for her daughters. Her voice was too weak from being choked and Slim didn't have time to wait. He snatched her by her neck and drug her from the room.

"Get off my mama!" Shay shouted as she punched his torso. Little David joined in but he didn't even register the kids as he drug their mother down the hall.

"The fuck going on!" Kirby snapped when he saw his mother being abused.

"The twins, where your sisters?" she pleaded. Kirby didn't hesitate since he had already been paid.

"They went to granny's house. Last night," he offered believably. So believably Slim believed him and slapped a spark out of Sheronda.

"Bitch I'll kill you 'bout my bread!" he swore. Kirby believed him and rushed to save his mother. He ran up hot and got knocked out cold.

"I told you I ain't got aghrgh!" she was saying before his hands wrapped back around her throat. Slim believed her too and lifted her off her feet by her neck. He pinned her against the wall, squeezing her throat and demanding his money.

"Give, me, my money, bitch!" Slim growled and squeezed as her feet kicked in the air. The younger kids pulled at his arms trying to dislodge their mother but were no effect. The man had blacked out while Kirby finally came to. He saw the situation had worsened and ran to his room.

"Let her go!" Kirby shouted and fired a round into the ceiling. That got Slim's attention but he was still choking his mama. "Let her go or I'ma shoot you in your face!"

"Shoot lil..." Slim was saying but Kirby cut him off. He kept his word and fired a bullet into his face.

Slim looked so confused but a bullet in the brain has that effect. He let Sheronda go since he has more pressing matters at hand. The end of his life came calling before he even fell to the ground. Sheronda beat him to the hardwood floor and her kids rushed to her side. He turned, took a step that would be his last and fell on his face. His blood rushed from the small hole in his face and formed a large pool around him.

"Mama! Mama!" Shay shouted while David shook. Meanwhile, Kirby just blinked as he processed what just happened. He had just killed a man in his hallway. There was more to process when he looked down at his mother. Her eyes were open but didn't see shit. Nor could she hear her babies telling her to wake up from where she was.

Slim was on his way to hell but would have company since he took Sheronda with him. They both had more company on the way.

"WELL HELLO THERE!" Sinclair slurred to a strange man who walked by her barstool perch.

"Yeah, no. Un-uh," he declined and shook his head. She may have forgotten taking him home a few weeks ago but he hadn't. The drunken sex was actually pretty good but there is too much pussy in Atlanta to hit the same one twice. He dismissed her in search of some new pussy.

"Hey there," a gentleman greeted as she slid into the adjacent barstool. It generally stayed empty since the regulars knew Sinclair was a mean drunk. Except when she was trying to get laid, like now.

"Hello yourself..." Sinclair replied and got stuck on the familiar face. Her face strained as she tried to place him. She was sure she knew him but couldn't quite place him. "Did we fuck?"

"No, but we can," he assured her.

"We can," she shot back and they both stood from their perches. Sinclair wobbled a little bit but he was there to make sure she didn't go down. At least not here, like that.

"You live near here?" he asked as they stepped out into the muggy night air.

"Right there!" she cheered and pointed at a nearby high rise. She twisted her lips at the building and changed her mind. Sinclair turned and pointed at the next high rise building and declared, "That one."

She wrapped her arm in his as they strolled a few blocks over. They were both relieved when her key worked in the lobby. An elevator ride later they emerged on her floor and made their way down the hall and inside.

"Come on Mr..." she growled and pulled him down the hall and into her bedroom. They quickly stripped down to their birthday suits and climbed on the bed. Sinclair leaned in for a kiss but he had a better idea.

"Here..." he said as he guided her head down below his

waist where a flaccid dick awaited. She gripped the soft dick in her hand and inspected it.

Sinclair approved and planted a loud kiss on the mushroom head. A few more kisses and licks and it began to grow. Soon she was working a full fledged erection in and out of her mouth. She had sucked more dick in the months following the divorce than she had during the twenty year marriage. As a result she had become quite efficient at it. Everyone is good at something and Sinclair was a certified cock sucker. It was no surprise when he began to writhe and moan.

"Mmhm," she hummed and increased her suction. She pumped the shaft a few times before he erupted in her mouth. She clamped down and let the hot lava run down her throat until he was spent, but still hard.

"Gotta excuse me. It's been a minute," he apologized for the quick nut as he reached for the rubber.

"No problem, as long as you know what to do with that!" she purred and laid back. Actions speak louder than words so he responded by shoving himself inside of her. Luckily she wasn't expecting any tenderness because she had none coming.

Some men change up after they get the pussy but this one changed as soon as he got inside of it. He scooped her legs under his elbows and nearly folded her in half. Sinclair gritted her teeth and gripped the sheets for the rough ride.

"Yeah bitch!" he snarled as he began beating the bottom of her box like an African drum. Sinclair wasn't sure how she felt about being called a bitch but knew for a fact she liked the beat he was producing. If she could rap she would have spit something to it.

"That's right. I'm a, bitch!" she screamed as he lifted her ass from the bed and dug even deeper. She was pretty sure he had reached her stomach but didn't mind.

The man growled and snarled as he literally mauled the pussy. His face began to twist and distort when the inevitable drew near. He picked up the pace and pounded with every ounce of his two hundred pounds of muscle concentrated into his dick. Sinclair barely beat him to the punch and nutted all over his dick. The resulting shivers and gush of juice pressed his detonator as well.

"Fuck!" he shouted and filled the rubber to the rim. He roughly snatched out of her just in case it didn't hold. The last thing he needed was to leave a trace behind.

"Whew!" Sinclair declared after the rough sex concluded with an explosive climax. The man collapsed on top of her and let her legs down. She let him catch his breath before moving or speaking. "Get up. Let me get a washcloth."

"Mmhm," he hummed and rolled off. He looked up and watched her round ass jiggle into the bathroom.

"Whew!" Sinclair repeated to her reflection and giggled. The dick had her giddy as she lathered up a washcloth. She had just wiped the puddle from between her legs when the man appeared in the mirror behind her.

"Mmhm," he hummed and wrapped his arm around her neck from behind.

"Mmmm," she hummed, closed her eyes and leaned on to the dick pressing into her back.

"You never asked my name," he reminded as his dick began to throb.

"Because I..." Sinclair began and froze when her eyes opened again. The excellent lighting in her mirror shed light on the familiar face. She realized the danger and tried to pull away, but the strong forearm tightened and held her in place.

"Mmhm, you know exactly who I am , don't you?" he dared and tightened some. "They used to call me Big Marquis cuz I had a son. Lil Marquis, until y'all took him away from me."

Sinclair felt her oxygen began to deplete from the constant pressure. She began to claw at his arm when her feet came off the ground. Marquis ignored the gouges in his forearm and continued. "First, your son killed my boy. Then your husband takes my bitch. I was supposed to fuck Marquita, not you."

Sinclair couldn't concentrate on the words because concentration requires oxygen and she had none. She felt herself on the verge of blacking out and fought to stay conscious.

'Mommy! I'm waiting for you' her son's voice called from the blurry distance. 'Come on mommy'

"I'm coming Carey," Sinclair said in her mind and went limp. Marquis kept on squeezing as her feet dangled above the tile floor. She was good and dead before he dumped her in the tub and walked away.

"One down, one to go..." he said on his way out of the apartment. "Finna kill the husband too. And take err thang that I got coming!"

The End

"Sup?" Vonda asked when she answered the knock on the door and found Latisha standing there. She wasn't alone since a grim faced woman stood beside her. Something told her it wasn't business and whatever it was, wasn't good.

"Can we come in" she asked on behalf on them both but Vonda sense the stranger would be staring in this show. She stepped aside so they could enter.

Latisha let her eyes give a quick inspection to make sure the girl was on point. They were all making good money from their hustle but she needed to make sure the young woman wasn't flossing. Flossing will get you knocked and locked quicker than anything.

Vonda saw her eyes jet around the apartment and gave herself a pat on the back for being smarter than that. She did enough flossing when she didn't have shit so now she just stacked her bread. What little cash she carried was carried in a knockoff purse. The used Lexus she drove was older than her and about right for a college kid. The rest was getting stacked.

"Sup?" Vonda repeated since she wasn't answered the first time. She directed this one to the other woman since it was her show.

"I'm detective Stanley, homicide," she said and paused to produce her badge. Vonda braced herself since homicide detectives are usually the bearers of bad news.

"Who got kilt?" she croaked.

"It was your mom," Latisha jumped in since the detective was being dramatic. She had done this enough to know to just get to it. Just snatch the bandaid off and let them deal with the pain.

"My mom?" Vonda asked with what could have been a chuckle. Not that it was funny, she just wondered what took it so long.

"Yes. Sheronda Perry was killed in her home. Your grandmother said she can take the younger kids," Stanley explained.

"Can you take care of your older sisters?" Latisha asked softly.

"Huh? Oh, yeah. Sure," she answered before thinking because that's what family does. Except she remembered what else family does when the twins jumped her. Her hand went to the faint remnant of the gash Panda scratched into her face. That face began to move from side to side as she thought about it. "As a matter of fact, naw fuck them hoes. They for the streets, let the streets have em..."

STAY TUNED for the finale in volume 4....

Black Ink Publications Presents

LOVES, LIES & LACEFRONTS
A SOUTHERN LOVE STORY

A Novel

By

Sa'id Salaam

"Girl, let me see what he working with!" Shandera fussed as she took Bella's phone out of her hand. The animated woman was always fussing whether she was happy or sad, melancholy or mad. Part of her theatrics were a frown, grimace or twisted lip at whatever was going on at the moment.

At this moment, they were discussing Bella's latest suitor; well, his dick, anyway. There were plenty of conversations at Bella's beauty salon but most had something to do with somebody's dick. Even a conversation about the pastor's latest sermon would somehow get a dick in it. Food, dick. The weather, dick. Music, dick. Dick, dick, dick the long day through.

"Damn, girl!" Bella complained about her snatching her phone away. She may have been the boss but most times, she was one of the girls. She put a hand on her shapely hip and batted her greyish eyes in mock protest. Technically, her French, Indian and African American mix made the girl a mutt, but it came together to form an exotic beauty that turned heads everywhere she went. She couldn't keep a man, though, which explained the new dick pic in her phone.

"I know that's right! I needs to see the dick up front!" Alexis huffed. The big woman was fronting, though, because she couldn't take any dick anyway. The average six-inch variety would have her whooping and hollering like an Indian on the warpath.

"It's the little dicks you gotta look out for! All four of my baby daddies got little dicks," a customer added from Shandera's chair.

The hairdresser stayed in hot demand due to her skills and vibrant personality. She was a name brand to be dropped, like Prada or Gucci. She only played second fiddle to Bella, who was widely regarded as the best hairdresser in the city, if not state, East of the mighty Mississippi, have her tell it. There was a rivalry right beneath the epidermis of their friendship but it was to be expected since every Jesus needs a Judas. It's the cost one paid to be the boss. And being the boss meant you just had to stay on guard for the inevitable cross.

"Eh, it's okay. No bumps or bruises. Nice curve, good veins," Shandera said as she analyzed the prospective penis. She turned and twisted the phone to view the dick from different angles. The woman was an expert after all when it came to dicks. A dick-ologist, if you will. "Seven, maybe eight inches. If he know how to work it, you may be in business."

"Chile, let me see this thang!" Sherbert, the resident sissy, hissed like sissies do.

He then rubbed his big hands on his apron and came over to inspect. "Mm-hm...un-huh...I know him! Dennis

McDaniels, age 32, lives at 25 Lafayette Court in the 7th Ward."

All mouths gaped at the news, except for Bella, that is. She just shook her head and laughed. The girls often sicced the sissy on any guy they thought about getting serious with. A sad fact was that a lot of the men out there would fuck with a man if they could get away with it. Only the owner of this particular penis wasn't named Dennis and he wasn't from 7th Ward.

"Eeehh! Wrong answer!" Bella buzzed like a game show. "That ain't him and he ain't from here!"

That was all they were getting out of her about her long-distance lover. They were still cultivating each other after meeting on social media a few months ago. The subject finally got around to sex, hence the dick pic. Most dudes will shoot one off in a second to a woman's inbox. Not Gavin. No; he took it slow.

"But, how you know that's really his? Dudes catfish dicks, you know," Alexis threw in, and she was right. Some will catfish a whole body and photoshop their head on it. Yes, it's deceptive, but so are contacts and lace fronts. Those may not be his pecs or abs, but some women don't look nothing like their pictures, either. Many a man have taken a woman home only to wake up to another one."

"Girl, what kind of man would have pictures of another man's penis in his phone?" Bella demanded to know in a WTF tone.

"Um...right here, Chile!" Sherbert raised a hand and waved.

The whole shop cracked up and cackled in laughter. No matter how miserable life could be on the outside, the shop was always good for a laugh. There were plenty of tears as well.

"My point exactly," Bella cosigned.

"Oh yeah, Sherbert, what's up with ole boy I asked you about?" Baby Girl asked hopefully. The nineteen-year-old had just completed cosmetology school and landed her job at the hottest salon in New Orleans. The job was part luck, part charity since Bella knew her mother from around The Ward. Her story was similar to her own, so she had to show love.

Angelique's mother, Demetria, had her at fourteen, by sixteen she was using dope, and was dead by seventeen, leaving her baby girl behind. The whole hood adopted the baby and dubbed her Baby Girl. The hood stood up and got her through high school and then cosmetology school. Baby Girl had a penchant for the bad boys she grew up around. Luckily for her, she had Sherbert and the rest of the gang to school her on them.

"Who, Slugga? He gay!" he nodded in agreement as he whipped out his phone with the proof. They always wanted proof when it was a dude they really liked. Even though sometimes that didn't stop some if they really, really liked a guy. It was one of the reasons the HIV rate was so high in the city. Another was the constant tourism that helped diseases flow to and fro, far and wide. People came for Mardi Gras and left with a lot more than beads. In the city's defense, plenty of those tourists arrived with diseases of their own, trading STDs like baseball cards.

"Damn shame!" Baby girl fumed, seeing the goon with dreads and gold teeth butt-naked in the sissy's phone. His jailhouse fine frame was covered in crude tats, adding to his ghetto appeal. He was gay, though, so, "You can have him."

"I already did! You can get him back," Sherbert laughed twice, once at his little joke and again at the look of utter disgust on the young girl's face. It was exactly the reaction she should have had.

She made a big production out of deleting his number from her phone and him from her life. Bella nodded her head in approval, as it was the reaction she expected. She couldn't watch the girl forever. She may own the hottest salon in the city, but she was making plans to leave.

"Girl, how you end up with a building in the French Quarter anyway?" a newer patron asked, knowing that the buildings in the gentrified city were worth millions and Bella was barely thirty.

"Oh boy!" Shandera groaned playfully even though she was serious. She had heard the story about Bella's grandmother a hundred times already. This would make a hundred and one as Bella fondly recalled the come up of the woman who raised her.

"My Grandma was a bad bitch back before bitches was supposed to be bad. A hustler fo' real..."

"Monsieur Beufonte, the new cook is here," the maid announced with a timbre of fear in her voice. She should be scared, after what happened with the last cook. The one who got chased out of the estate with a butcher knife in her back and her panties at her ankles...

Made in the USA
Columbia, SC
23 August 2022